In 1965
and Other Stories

In 1965
and Other Stories

by
Albert Robida

Translated, annotated and introduced by
Brian Stableford

A Black Coat Press Book

Visit our website at www.blackcoatpress.com

ISBN 978-1-61227-728-8. First Printing. February 2018. Published by Black Coat Press, an imprint of Hollywood Comics.com, LLC, P.O. Box 17270, Encino, CA 91416. All rights reserved. Except for review purposes, no part of this book may be reproduced or transmitted in any form or by any means, electronic or mechanical, including photocopying, recording, or by any information storage and retrieval system, without permission in writing from the publisher. The stories and characters depicted in this novel are entirely fictional. Printed in the United States of America.

TABLE OF CONTENTS

Introduction

"En 1965" by Albert Robida, here translated as "In 1965," was originally published as a ten-part *feuilleton* serial in *Les Annales politiques et littéraires* between 26 October 1919 and 18 January 1920 (there was no episode in the 14 December issue, which was the special Christmas number). It was the only long story in Robida's series of quasi-futurological visions of life in the mid-twentieth century that was not reprinted in book form. The same periodical had previously published a pair of vignettes by Robida, "L'Automobilisme en 1950" and "L'Aviation en 1950" in the 27 December 1908 issue, and Robida was presumably commissioned to write "En 1965" as an extended companion-piece; the two items are translated here, as "Motoring in 1950" and "Aviation in 1950," in order to provide prologues to the serial. The second novella added to the present volume as a makeweight, *L'île des centaures*, was originally published in 1912 by Henri Laurens, and was reprinted in 1931.

The present volume is the sixth volume of translations of works by the writer and illustrator Albert Robida (1848-1926) to be published by Black Coat Press, following *The Clock of the Centuries* (2008; also containing "Yesterday Now"), *The Adventures of Saturnin Farandoul* (2009), *Chalet in the Sky* (2011; also containing "A Schoolboy in 1950"), *Electric Life* (2013) and *The Engineer von Satanas* (2015; also containing both versions of "War in the Twentieth Century"). Collectively, the six volumes contain all of his contributions to the genre of *roman scientifique* except *Le Vingtième siècle* (1883) a translation of which was published as *The Twentieth Century* by Wesleyan University Press in 2004.

Perhaps the most remarkable thing about "En 1965" is its stark contrast to Robida's previous futuristic novel, the grim apocalyptic fantasy *L'Ingénieur von Satanas*, published earlier in 1919. That novel had been a radical break from the futurological series constituted by *Le Vingtième siècle*, *La Vie électrique* (*La Science Illustrée* 28 November 1891-30 July 1982; book 1892; tr. as Electric Life) and "Un Potache en 1950" (*Mon Journal* 8 September-22 December 1917; tr. as "A Schoolboy in 1950"), and "En 1965" was, in effect, a return to that "main sequence" of his futuristic visions.

L'Ingénieur von Satanas had, however, been a continuation of a spinoff series consisting specifically of visions of future warfare, which had begun with one of the episodes in his long chronicle of the *Voyages très extraordinaires de Saturnin Farandoul dans les 5 ou 6 parties du monde et dans tous les pays connus et meme inconnus de M. Jules Verne* (1879; tr. as *The Adventures of Saturnin Farandoul*), in which Saturnin Farandoul and Phileas Fogg end up on opposite sides in a war fought between the North and South of the Disunited States of Nicaragua, in which heavily armored "locomotives of war" (i.e., giant tanks) mount fearsome charges, gigantic cannons launch unprecedentedly powerful shells, "submarine cavalry" mount a daring raid to capture the transatlantic cable, and chloroform bombs play a crucial role, before a climactic battle takes place between two fleets of war-balloons.

Many of those images of future warfare cropped up again in a short documentary story that Robida wrote as a kind of advertisement for Le Vingtième siècle, "La Guerre au vingtième siècle," which appeared in the 27 October 1883 issue of the magazine he edited, *Le Caricature*. A different short story with the same title was published as an illustrated book by Georges Decaux in 1887, reiterating much of the same imagery in a different geographical context. Although the detail of the author's anticipations had only been slightly modified in *L'Ingénieur von Satanas* to take aboard the scientific and technological innovations of the intervening years—many of which he had anticipated—his attitude to the prospects in question had shifted markedly, the tone of wry black comedy adopted in the stories from the 1980s with one of furiously bitter criticism and dire pessimism.

None of that is visible in "En 1965," which is a conscientiously amicable and breezy work, with only a slight macabre edge in its comedy—considerably slighter than the trenchant satire of *La Vie électrique*, the technological innovations of which it recapitulates and updates faithfully, and also slighter than the ominous implications of the final work in the sequence, *Un Chalet dans les airs* (1925; tr. as "Chalet in the Sky"), which was written for a juvenile audience, like "Un Potache en 1950," but is markedly darker in the pattern of its anticipations. The history of the twentieth century sketched out in the previous texts is, of necessity, modified in order to accommodate the Great War, the aftermath of which plays a considerable part in the back-story of "En 1965," but there is no mention of the fundamental assumption of *L'Ingénieur von Satanas*, which is that the armistice of 1918 was merely an interruption, and that the war would soon resume, completing the total obliteration of civilization. Obviously, in the 1965 envisaged by the new story, that could not have happened, but it seems, on the contrary to be a world from which war has been completely banished, apparently having become unmentionable as well as unthinkable.

The reason for that drastic change of tack, and the consequent extreme moderation, is presumably that "En 1965" was commissioned by Adolphe Brisson, the editor-in-chief of *Les Annales politiques et littéraires*, and the author was writing in accordance with a specific instruction to maintain a light tone appropriate to a Parisian society many of whose members wanted to put the terrible legacy of the Great War firmly behind them, and to look forward resolutely to better times that might lie ahead. Brisson must have had the two 1908 vignettes very much in mind, and presumably requested that their themes be extrapolated in a kindred spirit.

Brisson's editorial pressure was probably also responsible for the fact that the plot of the serial seems to betray its initial robust political intentions, and to conclude in a fashion that is bound to seem craven to modern feminists. One suspects that the author cannot have planned that himself, and that the forced dereliction of intent might have been partly responsible for the fact that the text and its illustrations remained unreprinted.

Because its plot veers so awkwardly off course, "En 1965" is undoubtedly the weakest component of the twentieth-century series, but its futurological elements remain interesting, and introduced several significant innovations to supplement the imagery of the telephonoscope and the multiple social adaptations to the commonplace use of private aircrafts featured in *La Vie électrique*. Some of those innovations, notably the flying houses first mentioned in passing in "L'Automobilisme en 1950," were to be further developed in *Un Chalet dans les airs*. The Sacred Forest is an intriguing idea, albeit very much of its time, and the snapshots of underwater tourism are striking, although the porpoise-hunt would no longer be considered politically correct. The depiction of synthetic food reproduces an idea already broached extensively by other writers of *roman scientifique*, but does so in a suitably flamboyant fashion.

The relative flaccidity of the plot of "En 1950" is hopefully somewhat compensated in the present volume by the translation of "L'Île des centaures," which is a more well-rounded and effective story, and a fine example of modern Gulliveriana. Although the central hypothesis of a centaur civilization is fanciful, the story qualifies fully as an item of *roman scientifique* because of the role played in the lot by the two centaur scientists, whose appalling conduct holds up a satirical mirror to some of the less savory features of the sociology of European science. In that regard, the story has something in common with Edmond Haraucourt's classic satire "Le Gorilloïde" (1904; tr. in the Black Coat Press collection *Illusions of Immortality* as "The Gorilloid"[1]), which might well have played some part in its inspiration.

The comedy in "L'Île des centaures," although much broader than that in "En 1965," is also considerably sharper. The two novellas do, however, share a similar utopian philosophy and sarcastic distaste for certain aspects of modern civilization, which unites them in spite of the drastic variance between the imagery of their backcloths and the markedly different narrative strategies required to accommodate those different kinds of

---

[1] ISBN 978-1-61227-075-3.

imagery. That combination of similarity and contrast enables the two novellas to form an interesting, appealing and eminently readable diptych.

The translation of "En 1965" was made from the relevant issues of *Les Annales politiques et littéraires* reproduced on the Bibliothéque Nationale's *gallica* website. The translations of the two vignettes were made from the facsimile reproductions contained in the 1995 Apex Periodica edition of *La Locomotion Future*. The translation of *L'île des centaures* was made from the copy of the 1931 Laurens edition reproduced on the *gallica* website.

Brian Stableford

MOTORING IN 1950

What a beautiful sunny day the first Saturday in June 1950 was! The previous day's storm had cleared the atmosphere, the Great Central Station for the Capture of Atmospheric Energy having decanted all the energy from the north-eastern region—an economy for energy production—and everything was set fair for a fortnight. And I was very glad to grant myself two weeks of vacation near Bayeux with my friend B***, in order to forget a few headaches, nervous excitations, stomach troubles and other petty inconveniences of the hectic life we lead.

The boulevard was heaving—more traffic than other days, naturally, because it was Saturday. In spite of the good organization of the circulation, the crossing facilities, the stages detours at the intersections, the subterranean passages and the elevated refuges for vehicles parking, the causeway was vibrating and still too narrow, in spite of being considerably widened at the expense of the sidewalks—which were almost useless, since there are no longer any of those insupportable pedestrians who used to clutter up the roads of olden days.

In the auto with my friend we threaded a path through the middle of the host of vehicles: merchants' delivery vehicles, picturesque in form by virtue of habit, adopted by way of advertisement, of arranging the vehicle in a form symbolizing the kind of industry or commerce; heavier autotrucks; elegant autocabs; family limousines, autofiacres; electric tricycles; light and coquettish autobuses; autocoupés and various autocars. All of that was flowing in two files, without any disorder, in truth, without the infernal obstructions at intersections that people used to curse so much, and almost without the disk-agents in tricars posted every twenty-five meters, who had too many opportunities to raise their white detonation-stocks to call some driver to order.

"And people once claimed that motoring was a sport!" said my friend. "It was a sport fifty years ago, like aviation, in the days of the conquistadors of the road and the atmosphere; but today, it's just the practical utilization of new forces."

We went past the elevators of the aerial station in the Boulevard Haussmann. All those people! Half way up, some were taking the suburban electric tubes[2] for Rouen, Tours or Compiègne, others were going all the way up to the embarkation platform of the airships for Brittany, Normandy, the Vosges and the Midi.

"Look out!" I said. "Let's try not to receive anything on our heads—there are so many people who might drop a trunk, or a simple umbrella."

"Get away! Distracted people in today's society? There are none left—they were all crushed before reaching the age of fifteen. Dreamers and poets? The last ones were suppressed in 1910 or 1912 by the crushbuses of those days, in the explosion crisis of the great congested

---

[2] By "tubes" Robida means a large-scale version of the kind of pneumatic tubes then used in Paris as an alternative postal service, in which small packages were impelled by compressed air. A memorable journey through a passenger-carrying tube of that sort is described in "Un Potache en 1950," and they are a significant background feature of "En 1965."

cities. Don't worry, though, verses get made just the same. No worries! My son and daughter are coming back from school in their usual little auto—an autoflea, as it's known—one from Sévigné-Pontoise, the other from Condorcet-l'Isle Adam. They'll take the eight thirty-five airship and arrive at the villa at about ten o'clock..."

We rolled for a long time through open country on the rubber road, behind many other people going to their country houses at various distances from busy Paris. We could already see trees. We crossed paths with market gardeners' autocars brings their vegetables to Les Halles, sometimes from a long way away, removal autos carrying furniture to country houses, a long fifty-seat autocar taking a company of anglers to Caudebec, even longer autocars taking schoolchildren from Paris to spend a long weekend in the woods, and numerous limousines loaded with families of shopkeepers—father, mother, children, sons-in-law, daughters-in-law, cousins of both sexes, etc. I even saw a little carriagette carrying a lady and gentlemen already clad in shrimp-fishing costumes, with their nets over the hood...

Further along there was a veritable convoy: twelve auto-trucks laden with sacks of flour; then we went through a returning free market, fat farmers in their little autos, grocers' and butter-merchants' trucks and a few cows on an autotrolley. Then, installed on one side of the road, near a charming river, camping enthusiasts, five or six auto-caravans or housecars making their tour of France, disdaining hotels: a charming tableau, the kitchens fuming, ladies in bright dresses setting trestle-tables, children playing...and tomorrow they would all be camping two hundred kilometers away, in another pretty location...

Finally, as night is falling, we arrive. The Cherbourg tube is passing over a viaduct; we can hear the hum of electric trains inside. Up above, a few dirigibles are cleaving the air, going to scatter among the coastal resorts; the sea is shining ahead of us. Here come the woods, a long line of cliffs, lighthouses illuminating, and here's the villa that will shelter us for a few days...

AVIATION IN 1950

"Oof! Let's take off our goggles and fur coats."

"Sapristi! Let's have a look at the *Telejournal*... Hello! Hello! Questions were asked in the Chamber today. The Minister of Highways and Aerial and Terrestrial Communications was on the spot...a matter of rubberization. The Midi's demanding...we'll see. Hello! Hello!"

*Lively discussion...virulent speech by...*drinn, drinn, let's skip the speeches... *Motion of censure...1,246 votes to 342...* That's it, the Ministry has gone off the rails...

In the air, at the aerial bar of an electric station. Down below, a few autos are stationed, recharging their accumulators. Half way up, under the big hangars, and garages, various vehicles are waiting: a little hired dirigible, two airbuses, three airplanes and a balloonette.

Three gentlemen, two ladies and three children aged between ten and fifteen are finishing lunch. The weather is superb, the sun is shining. People are talking about the previous day's storm.

"Only four accidents, one quite serious..."

"There are so many imprudent people, young men who launch fourth, in order to show off, in racing airplanes, and other poor devils, on the contrary, for want of money, in four-sou contraptions devoid of solidity, nailed together any old how! Parents really ought to keep better watch on those refugees from college."

"Oh, my dear, nowadays, since they do flying and gliding at school, as my grandfather used to do canoeing…anyway, Gaston here, if he passes his bac next year, I'll by him a little twelve-hundred-franc airdart; he'll be able to take reasonable little trips. He knows how to drive, too, going out in the dirigible every Sunday. He has his pilot's license…"

"That's not too dusty!" said young Gaston.

"Oh, no, Papa!" say the two girls in chorus.

"Look at that old worm-eaten airboat arriving from the south-south-east. What an antique! It must date back to 1930! They built things to last in those days."

"But it's scarcely moving. Look, it's crossing paths with the Saint-Malo autobus; it needs an effort of the engine to avoid a collision…"

"By the way, did you hear what happened last week in the forest of Fontainebleau, beyond Barbizon? Thieves brought off a double coup. They'd just burgled a big villa by forcing the door of the upper landing pad— the owners were at the theater in Paris—and they were flying over the forest with their loot when their dirigible encountered a tourist plane going to Italy for a honeymoon trip. Harpooning! Terror! The poor fellow tried to resist, but the young lady fainted. Robbed of everything in two minutes!"

"Well, thieves have a good time with planes, in spite of all the surveillance…"

"It's the same for smuggling. Might as well get rid of the customs…"

"You know how marvelous a plane is for discovering in monuments beauties unknown to spectators on the ground! Well, there are indelicate people who abuse that.

They unbolt highly-perched statues. An Englishman was arrested the other day who, under the pretext of admiring Reims cathedral, was carrying away souvenirs."

"Oh, these collectors!"

"Dear Madame, I saw something very droll three months ago in Egypt: races of gliders, airplanes and airdarts, with the pyramids as obstacles, to be jumped one after another. I did it, but I nearly caught a Bedouin as I came down. I avoided him by a sideways leap, bat my propeller broke on the head of the Sphinx. If business is good I'll go in November with an agency airship to spend twelve days hunting in Abyssinia…lions, panthers…"

"Oh!" said the young schoolboy, admiringly.

"Provided, of course, that there isn't a war between now and then. Airfleets are increasing everywhere. People are constructing, constructing…"

"It's necessary! Some Asiatic flotilla might fall upon us tomorrow without any warning. It's so easy, in spite of all our cruisers! A gust of wind, a series of mists in the atmosphere, a hitch in the advanced international patrols, and they're through. It's fine, aviation, but there's another side to the coin: general insecurity!"

"Personally, I'm planning to go to London on Thursday."

"In your airboat?"

"Oh, if it were a matter of going to New York I'd go by the transatlantic airship…"

"I don't travel much, myself. Oh, my friend, at night, coming out of the Opéra at the top, with all the planes going past or parked, the municipals, Paris, all illuminated…the costumes, the Tour Saint-Jacques in the distance, the Cloud-Palace, the Arc de Triomphe, the terraces of the restaurants, is worth more than the Alps from above or Venice in an airgondola, Constantinople, all the great spectacles... It's superb!"

IN 1965

*I. The Encumberment of the Parisian Sky
and its Disruptions of Circulation.
A Handbag Lost in an Airplane Jam*

Having lavished a dozen kisses on each of her two children—Gustave, a young fellow of six, already tall and determined, and Pierrette, a girl of five, with a pretty pink face beneath wild curls, seemingly sketched in flourishes by an eighteenth-century master with blue dots for eyes—Madame Suzanne Montgrabel finally seemed to calm down. She drank a glass of water, moistened her temples slightly, kissed her children another six times, threw herself into an armchair, got up, walked about agitatedly and sighed profoundly.

The chambermaid, who had been following the various phases of the scene for ten minutes, seemed reassured, and smiled.

"Truly, if Madame had not recovered completely, I could have believed that she had fallen eighteen hundred meters from the tower of Notre Dame! But Madame, it's only a trivial little accident, such as happens every day. These air-taxi pilots are so imprudent! They bump into everything! Adroit imprudence is forgivable, but clumsiness is understandably disagreeable. If Madame had taken her autoflyer, she would be in this state..."

"That's nothing," said Suzanne. "What annoys me is that I've lost my handbag, that's all..."

"Did Madame have her jewels in it, or her check book?"

"No, Annette, just a few papers..."

"Well, then, it's nothing."

Suzanne Montgrabel allowed some emotion to show again. It was a great deal for a trivial air-taxi accident such as happened every day—or rather, a simple incident of circulation. A little while ago, a hundred and fifty meters above Neuilly, her air-taxi, awkwardly caught between a minihydroplane and an autoflyer, had given her half a second of terror, but the air-taxi had got out of it by dropping downwards.

The usual airplane accident altercations had followed, her pilot was called a "carter" and a "bus-driver" by his colleagues—stinging but unimportant insults, immediately evaporated in the atmosphere by virtue of the speed of the vehicles. However, Suzanne, surprised or distracted, and in any case not very brave, had dropped her pretty little handbag overboard in her disturbance.

An unimportant loss, since it did not contain either jewelry or a check-book—but why, then, was Suzanne Montgrabel so upset, even anxious, over such a little inconvenience?

"My God!" she murmured, in a terrified tone, "what a disaster! Why did I...? What if it falls into my husband's hands? What shall I do! What shall I say? And my father-in-law! My God, what imprudence! No, no, it's necessary to get it back immediately...!"

She looked at her watch. The hands were not moving very quickly.

"It needs time—I don't want to go too soon. Oh, what if the bag has fallen in the Seine and sunk to the bottom! But no, it wasn't heavy enough; there was no jewelry in it, unfortunately. Let's see, what time is it? Let's wait a little longer..."

She toyed distractedly with little Pierrette's curls and gazed vaguely at a page of Gustave's handwriting. Then she picked up the telephone and rang the central flight terrace of the Montgrabel house—the flight-pad, as one says—for her personal pilot.

"Firmin, will you get the autoflyer ready—we're going out."

A few more words over the tele to Madams Montgrabel, her husband's mother: "I'm going out for a short trip, Mother dear, and I'll be back in no time."

"It's just," said Madame Montgrabel, in a slightly plaintive voice, "that it's one of my days of depression, you know...life is so busy! So much to do! It gives me vertigo...I still have ten reports on our social work to read, twenty-five accounts to check and thirty letters to dictate in the meantime... See you soon."

"I'll be back in no time, Mother dear."

At the flight-pad Suzanne found Firmin, who was starting up his engine; she only had to leap into the autoflyer.

"The Central Lost Property Office," she said.

23

The autoflyer took off without a jolt. It is a fine instrument, the autoflyer, a model so slim and so solid in its delicate appearance; it has three light wheels and takes off immediately at a simple pressure of the pilot's hand.[3] A slightly old-fashioned vehicle, undoubtedly, but

---

[3] Robida's illustration shows a vehicle with three wheels set in a linear arrangement, one in front of another. An "autoflyer" is a primarily a road vehicle, which employs its wings in order to jump over inconvenient obstructions—and idea that failed to catch on even in futuristic fiction, although similar vehicles

very convenient for short trips and much appreciated by timorous individuals who do not like high-altitude winds or are slightly fearful of the bewildering aerial circulation and the veritable clutter of the air above large cities.

People complain a great deal about that encumbrance, although it is inevitable, as had to be accepted along with its various inconveniences. Certainly, at many points in the Parisian sky, the circulation is difficult to regulate suitably, but how could it be otherwise, with the thousands of vehicles of every sort that fly over the Parisian agglomeration and its surrounding area above the first twelve hundred meters of altitude: the countless airships, airplanes, hydroplanes, minihydroplanes, helicopters and other varieties of the numerous family of great artificial birds, leading to traffic jams around local flight-pads or tube stations?

Between that intense aerial circulation and terrestrial circulation, still considerable for heavy transportation, there is the intermediary—which is to say, autoflyers avoiding obstacles and, it is necessary to consider, descents from on high, the vertical circulation that is, of course, very troublesome on occasion.

At the first leaps or glides of the autoflyer, Suzanne Montgrabel could not help casting a suspicious glance around, above and below her. As the weather was superb, with bright sunshine, the sky was very animated. The auto rolled for two minutes, bounding over a few blocks of streets or boulevards, and flew at fifty meters, soon going around the swarming terrace of the great Neuilly flight-pad.

---

are featured in Victor Margueritte's *Le Couple* (1924; tr. as *The Couple*, Black Coat Press, ISBN 978-1-6122-362-4).

There were lots of people about, many walking—the weather was so fine! Between two business-meetings, people were going hastily to inflate the lungs by means of rapid hops in the atmosphere, where the vivifying western breezes could be felt as soon as one reached five hundred meters.

But the pilot Firmin could not be called a bus-driver. He was skillful and vigilant; there was nothing to fear with him. He did not tangle with any autoflyer or collide with any chimney-pot which hurdling an unusually tall building. Only the vertical circulation could cause Suzanne any anxiety.

In the distance, the great Paris-New York-San Francisco dirigible could be seen casting off; it was the hour of the daily departure. Generally, the friends or relatives who have accompanied the passengers on board allow the dirigible to gain height in order to descend by parachute. Parachutes with auxiliary motors, for diagonal descents, are frequently used nowadays—they are so convenient! You can quit airplanes or dirigibles at will, and the parachute sets you down at the chosen location tranquilly, without a jolt. It is, however, a prerogative that is not without occasional inconveniences for distracted or inattentive people down below, who are not paying sufficient attention to vertical circulation and risk receiving the parachute-traveler on the head, or allowing themselves to be clipped in passing.

Distraction is the sole and veritable cause of the majority of atmospheric accidents, almost always so easy to avoid with vigilance and a cool head. In our epoch, is it acceptable to dream outdoors? Can we, who live plunged in the formidable turbulence of modern life, carried away at top speed by the incessant breathlessness of very complicated machinery, walk around like our ancestors, tranquilly letting our minds drift in the insouciant waves of untimely reverie, as dangerous to others as ourselves? The clumsiness of airplane pilots, amateur or professional, gets the blame. In truth, that is quite mistaken. They are not clumsy; it is the obsolete dreamers—poets, if you wish—people of another era, who are at fault. One does well to say: "So much the worse for them!" Unfortunately, it is often so much the worse for others.

So Suzanne, in spite of her preoccupations, kept watch on the sky. In fact, the Paris-New York dirigible was taking away a cinema-opera troupe, and the numerous friends of the troupe's stars, having concluded their adieux and handed over their bouquets, were now quitting the dirigible. Their shouts could be heard—*See you soon! Bon voyage! Have a nice trip! Au revoir! A tele call without fail every evening! Au revoir!*—a confused rumor that faded away amid the varied music of engines, distant murmurs or nearby purrs.

In all directions, parachutes began to cut through the atmosphere as the friends of the troupe left the vessel.

"Look out, Firmin! Several of them are coming toward us!"

Firmin smiled without making any reply. He never lost himself in a dream, and did not care about parachutes.

At the same moment, a valise went past, like a yellow meteorite. A dreamer in the dirigible up above had dropped it, doubtless while contemplating the cinema-opera stars.

"Oh!" said Suzanne.

That was more dangerous and les easily avoidable. Unfortunately, it is still necessary, in aerial life, for us to expect a certain amount of imprudence and negligence, which will certainly diminish over time. At every moment, a thousand objects rain down from the sky: poorly-secured luggage that has escaped, helmets, hats, flying packages, or even bottles that have stupidly been allowed to roll away. There are sanctions, lawsuits and fines, which are perhaps not severe enough.

By means of an abrupt serve, Firmin avoided the valise; he also avoided the maladroit gentleman who, in order not to lose it, had decided to follow it by parachute, postponing his journey until the next departure.

Five minutes later, the autoflyer landed in front of the Central Lost Property Office, annex 22 of the prefecture.

Suzanne got down quickly. It was vast, that Central Office: several halls where, behind a railed balustrade, one perceived a host of very various objects on tables, with labels and serial numbers. Suzanne passed them rapidly in review, searching for the hall of found objects of small dimension.

"But Madame," said the employee, when she had described the lost items at length, "it's too soon, too soon! We have hardly any of today's finds, as yet. It's necessary to wait until tomorrow..."

How annoying! Suzanne, increasingly desolate, went back to the autoflyer in order to return to the Montgrabel house. Frowning, her gaze distracted and irritated, she allowed herself now to be carried along without paying attention to the famous vertical circulation. Fortunately, she was not driving, and Firmin was inaccessible to distraction.

"I suspected that Madame would have a wasted journey," said the chambermaid Annette. "It was too soon. And then, one could have telephoned, since there was nothing in Madame's handbag..."

"Yes, yes...enough!" said Suzanne, to cut the matter short. "If, by any chance, it's returned, call me immediately."

Suzanne is the wife of Charles Montgrabel, the elder son of the great industrialist, whose many enormous and well-directed enterprises have earned him a worldwide celebrity. Charles Montgrabel, an engineer of red coal,[4] a man whose valor was already well-known, is absent at present. Studies in connection with the exploitation of volcanoes in Java and Sumatra have retained him in the Far East,

In order to perceive Monsieur Montgrabel, the head of the dynasty, we only have to cast a glance at the great hall of the staircase connecting the ten floors of the house, brightly illuminated laterally and also from above, by the daylight pouring through by the perforated tower bearing the airplane flight platform.

Magnificent in its architecture, that stairway of honor, superbly decorated, worthy of Versailles or the Château de Vaux-Fouquet, is broad enough to accommodate the maneuvers of a cavalry squadron, but it is as deserted as it is sumptuous, because no one ever goes up the steps or admires the decorations of its wrought-iron banisters. Only the elevators are employed.

---

[4] "Houille rouge" [red coal] was a phrase that had taken on a macabre meaning in France during the Great War, with reference to the blood whose spillage was fuelling the war. Robida is, therefore, making a joke in re-adapting it to a quasi-literal meaning; Charles is an industrial engineer employing red-hot lava inside volcanoes as a power source for electricity generation.

On the wall above the fist landing, facing the door of the hall, is a full-length portrait of Monsieur Montgrabel by a illustrious painter, as sumptuous in its color as the staircase: a portrait that gives the impression of being an equestrian portrait, so imposing is it, and so majestically do the eyes of the portraiture seem to float above over everything that the central portal allows to be perceive of Paris and the expanses of the sky that it opens up. But the portal is always shut. People generally enter the house via the terrace above it.

The portrait of Monsieur Montgrabel does not lie, and the authoritarianism of the model is well-known. The family knows something about that, as does everyone in the celebrated industrialist's entourage or employed in his enterprises.

Thus, without divining the cause, we can understand the emotion of Suzanne, who cannot help darting a glance in the direction of her father-in-law's portrait as she traverses the landing in order to reach the apartment of the elder Madame Montgrabel.

"Here I am, Mother dear," she says, on entering her mother-in-law's small office. Once, one would have said "boudoir," but nowadays one says "small office" or "study," for Madame Montgrabel is a very busy person and the small office is, in reality, a large and brightly-lit room, in which the luxurious desk laden with papers and the telephonoscope are framed by desks for typists and filing-cabinets of an almost administrative appearance instead of credenza, tapestries and display cases full of knick-knacks, as in olden days.

Madame Montgrabel, a rather robust and very elegant woman, whose features still display the residues of youth, is in the process of rummaging through the files and stacks of paper accumulated in her immense desk, searching for her mislaid spectacles. She stirs her papers, throws an armful of files on the floor, and finally unearths three pairs.

"Oof!" she says finally looking up at her daughter-in-law. "My dear child, you see a woman ravaged by cares. I can't do any more, and I'm going to revolt against your father-in-law's tyranny. He's been making me live a feverish existence of forced labor long enough! Take stock for a moment. I assume responsibility for the social relations of the enormous Montgrabel company— my husband doesn't have the time, of course—it's me who has to say to him: 'You know Philippe, Madame is our dear intimate friend... the gentleman near the fireplace is our very amiable country neighbor the Duc de X***, etc., etc." Fine! But in addition, I have to supervise the social affairs, masculine or feminine, created around our various factories, mines, enterprises and exploitations in the four corners of the world. As if the world only had four corners! But it has many more, and Monsieur Montgrabel always has something to found, undertake or reconstitute almost everywhere. Then I have to rack my brains and liquefy my brain, for the establishment and efficient functioning of gardens and crèches, schools, libraries, kitchen gardens and workers' parks, cooperatives, hospitals, insurance schemes, etc., etc. All well and good! But now, here are reports in Annamite: 'Workers' Housing in Tonkin,' where we have mines, 'Dispensary at Sontay.' Will I have to learn Tonkinese and Cambodian?"

II. In which Madame Montgrabel, in her day of depression, recalls memories of her beautiful seasons.

Madame Montgrabel picked up an armful of files, lost her spectacles, tried another pair, and broke a lens or two; she shifted papers urgently, threw some into her desk drawers, or the filing cabinets to the right and left, and then, putting down her four pair of spectacles, let herself collapse on to a chaise longue beside the armchair in which Suzanne was sitting, forcing herself to smile.

"I'm always talking about your frivolity," said Madame Montgrabel. "However, you seem to me to be have been worried for some time; I've noticed it. The health of the children isn't giving us any cause for concern, for the moment, so I conclude that it's our husband's perpetual absences that are making you pensive. The worthy Charles, always away on business, in Java or Cairo or elsewhere... Truly, Suzanne, I'm worried about you. I think you've changed recently; you go out a great deal but your friends complain about not seeing enough of you..."

Madame Montgrabel sighed profoundly.

"As I told you," she went on, "I'm in one of my days of depression. I dream of a few weeks of rest, a month—no, four months—of sweet idleness. To yawn a little! To become bored! To hear to more mention of enterprises, mines, factories, electricity, metallurgy...oh, what a dream! Yes, and summer is already well advanced..."

"Of, scarcely begun, Mother dear, scarcely begun..."

"Yes! Yes! And Monsieur Montgrabel won't consent to perceive it. I'm tormented, he has new projects that he doesn't want to talk about, which he'll only expose when he thinks the time has come...I'm suspicious. What is he preparing? Me I can't take it, I declare that I'm overwhelmed by too many things and I'm thinking of revolt! I think about my summer seasons, my beautiful summer seasons. How have I employed them—or, rather, how has Monsieur Montgrabel made me employ them, those beautiful seasons?"

"I know, Mother dear. You've already told me..."

"Do you think so? I never complain, though. Do you know, in the early years of our marriage, about the honeymoon voyage that we undertook after five or six years of marriage? Do you know how we employed it, that belated honeymoon, awaited for so long? A rapid journey through the oil-bearing regions of Rumania and Russia! Yes, Suzanne, a study of exploitations, wells and reserves! No palatial hotels, my child, gypsy huts...with all their inconveniences. What do you say to that? And famine added to fatigue! I lost two kilos a week. What a honeymoon! And I had to serve as Monsieur

Montgrabel's secretary, remember figures, makes notes of conversations, understand—or guess—all sorts of things... Oh, don't smile!"

"But I sympathize with you, Mother dear."

"Four weeks like that in remote lands. And for the end of that lovely wedding voyage, as a bouquet, Monsieur Montgrabel's ill humor, because the observations of our excursion didn't measure up sufficiently to his desires. A failed affair, he renounced it! I was worn out, at the end of my tether, he was exhausted, grumbling all the way home. A fine honeymoon!"

"Mother dear, I suspect you of regretting, like me, the sunlit days of a hundred or a hundred and fifty years ago..."

"Certainly! But perhaps you think that if our honeymoon was mightily spoiled, I was able to make up for it in the following seasons? Yes, shouldn't Monsieur Montgrabel, having become one of the great industrialists of France, and then of Europe, have tried to make me forget the initial disasters in the delights of an extraordinarily brilliant and marvelously organized existence? Oh, yes! What about the study of all the social questions attached to his enterprises? For I began, from then on, to direct affairs. But let's only talk about the periods of relaxation, our fine vacations! Last year, 1964, you were here, you recall the seductive program. It should have been delightful, that restful cruise in a hydrodirigible over the coast of Norway, with ports of call in all the fjords, long walks at the foot of vertiginous cliffs, or in the great fir woods, in the silence of somber forests..."

"Yes, yes, two days in the fjords, where, in any case, the forests have been cut down, and then the hydrodirigible takes us to freeze for three weeks in Iceland, between the icebergs and the glaciers, to study a big deal! Always the red coal, but volcanoes that don't warm. A failed deal, anyway, stolen by the Swedish Energy and Heat Company...Monsieur Montgrabel furious...!"

"Oh, how cold I was!" said Suzanne.

"And previously—you weren't there then, it was before your marriage—there was another fine holiday season! That time, Monsieur Montgrabel had put on the program: no voyage, rest cure in Normandy, in the heart of old France! We were to stay for six weeks under the apple trees, in the hay, the flowers of the fields, the grass of the meadows. Yes, yes! Fundamentally, it was a matter of the work of broadening the channel from Paris to the sea...construction-yards to establish, administrative difficulties to settle, conferences with prefects, sub-prefects and bridge-engineers. A battle of engineers! Fifty of ours launched to the assault! What a campaign! 'What are you complaining about?' said Monsieur Montgrabel. 'You vacation has been extended. Instead of the six weeks anticipated, we've stayed for two months!'"

Madame Montgrabel was uttering such profound sighs that Suzanne, sympathizing, almost forgot her handbag.

"I don't know yet where we're going this year, but it doesn't matter; I promise you that you'll be delighted, Mesdames," said a man's voice behind Suzanne, who shuddered in her armchair.

Madame Montgrabel, still plaintive and sighing, did not budge, but Suzanne turned round.

It was the telephonoscope behind her that had just spoken...

Suzanne saw Monsieur Montgrabel himself leaning forward, his face enlarged, on the large crystal screen of the apparatus, on which the interlocutors of tele conversations appeared, in perfectly clear images rather than the tremulous ones of the early days.

"I've been here for a quarter of an hour," he said. "It's a great pleasure to stir the memories of past summers like this, but it excites you so much that you don't hear the tele bell. I understand your desire very well. In any case, I'm like you, I have aspirations to calm, to solitude in nature. I sigh for repose! So, I've been here for fifteen minutes, waiting for the opportunity to get a word in, but you didn't give me time. So we're going to chat tranquilly about what's preoccupying you. As I said, our desires are concordant. I'm going to settle everything, and you'll be delighted, utterly delighted, this time—you'll see! I can't leave my office, I'm expecting a couple of calls... So, as I was saying, like you, I experience a veritable thirst for the open air, for...but someone's calling...my agent in Lyon...oh, business! Just a moment, I beg you..."

A brief gesture, a Jovian frown, and Monsieur Montgrabel disappeared abruptly from the tele.

He truly was the man of the great portrait, the authoritarian leader: tall and robust, with a full and red face, a long and forceful nose—a commanding nose, that always seemed ready to plunge forward, an "attacking nose," as his former chiefs of staff said, who knew him well and divined solely by the movement of that nose, what decisions to take. Monsieur Montgrabel's beard was still black, without a hint of dye, and his hair was scarcely retreating over his temples. He dressed in a jacket with a wide opening; the pockets to the right and left of the breast protruded, full of notebooks and wallets, each reserved for a certain order of business. The paper within remained almost blank, however, for Monsieur Montgrabel contented himself, instead of long notes, with scribbling hieroglyphs indecipherable for anyone else and for him; fortunately, rather than those cryptographic notebooks, he could be proud of his extra-solid memory, in which the smallest details of things that interested him were deeply engraved for all eternity, or very nearly.

Madame Montgrabel watched her husband disappear from the tele screen, and turned to her daughter-in-law.

"Aspirations for calm, and the sweetness of repose," she said. "I've always heard him say that when it's a matter of launching himself into some big deal...that worries me..."

"No, Mother dear, he seemed genuinely desirous of a little rest..."

"No, no, I remember! Thus, one year when he claimed to be absolutely exhausted by the turmoil of excessively numerous affairs, he had me organize and prepare, with great difficulty, every detail of an autumn season on Lake Chad. I would have preferred the Italian lakes, but her refused...too familiar, the Italian lakes, while Chad...and do you know, my child, that it was simply a matter of the purchase of warehouses, docks or factories of rubber, cocoa, palm oil, etc., and a general transformation of all those establishments... I was counting on spending a fine tranquil season on our comfortable air-pinnace, in a nice brand new bathing resort nestling between the giant trees of an immense park...as now, I was in my days of depression, but it was necessary to run from one shore of Chad to the other, to establishments almost always located in torrid or marshy places...and mosquitoes...and crocodiles, my child, crocodiles around our pinnace!"

"Always exaggerating!" exclaimed the voice of Monsieur Montgrabel.

This time, Monsieur Montgrabel was no longer in the tele; it was not his image but his person that lifted up the door-curtain of the room and arrived like an impetuous gust of wind.

"I protest! There were only a dozen, at the most, of those crocodiles, which came uniquely to give us the pleasure of shooting them. But it's no longer a matter of all that today—all that ancient history is no longer of any account. I have great news to announce to you, Mesdames, news that will lift you out of your dejection and depression immediately, make all the nervous troubles of which you're complaining disappear, my poor dear love, and will also give you great pleasure, little scatterbrained and frivolous Suzanette, gracious specimen of the genteel ladies of times past!"

"News?" said Madame Montgrabel, sitting up in her armchair.

"Aha! That's woken you up—already you're not so languid! Well, this is the news: I...my resolution is made, I've decided, it's settled..."

"Come on, don't keep us in suspense. What new great enterprise are you going to announce to me?"

"Wait for it! I've decided...to give up business! I've decided to hand on the torch! I've decided to let go of everything! In a word, I'm abdicating. Can't you see that I'm exhausted, depressed and languishing myself? You haven't noticed that?"

Monsieur Montgrabel struck his breast with a few solid blows of the fist.

"Yes, my children, it's settled, agreed with myself. I've already said a few words about it to my successors..."

"Is this serious?" stammered Madame Montgrabel.

"Is it serious? It's settled with my successors, I tell you. The company will become Montgrabel Sons, Daughters- and Sons-in-law. I'm going to invite them all: Charles, who's returning from Java today, Edouard, Maurice, Henriette, etc.—all of them, in order to hand over the helm of the Montgrabel ship to them, saying to them: 'Your turn, now! It's up to you to make progress, to continue the movement. Me, I count on living henceforth a life of total repose, living like a petty rentier, yawning in the sun!' What do you say to that, Madame? Are you satisfied? Look! Simply by virtue of having told you, I feel completely cheered up! Oh, hang on! Just a couple of words to say to someone..."

Monsieur Montgrabel launched himself to the tele, rang, and shouted a series of numbers. Half a minute later, a bell replied and something flickered on the screen.

Madame Montgrabel and Suzanne looked at one another.

"Excuse me—just a couple of words to the Anzin Power Station," said Monsieur Montgrabel. "There! We're off..."

The tele screen seemed to vibrate, light up and quiver. Becoming gradually more precise, like a fantastic apparition, there was a landscape of factories bristling with enormous chimneys, iron pylons, extraordinary buildings in which elevators overhung groups of tall towers, reminiscent of colossal and menacing steel Bastilles: massive blast-furnaces, reddened at the base by infernal mouths, forming something more than mere volcanoes.

Something akin to a distant and continuous low hum emerged from it, profound breaths, the muffled noise of pile-drivers or other titanic machines, and smoke, accompanied by red fumaroles, which rolled and swirled on the screen, seemingly about to invade Madame Montgrabel room, so convincingly that poor Suzanne was already coughing and clutching her throat.

The image became fixed. In a lighter cloud of smoke, a kind of vast office could be distinguished, with employees in the background, and electrical stations and consoles. There was a large window open over a cluttered canal, with the silhouettes of bizarre buildings in which flames flickered, and then the face of a man sitting at the apparatus, in the foreground.

The conversation had already started.

"Monsieur Crouzat, chief engineer of Anzin Power Station," said Montgrabel, sketching an introduction without turning round.

The two interlocutors were speaking loudly almost shouting, in order to overcome the incessant metallic racket out there. It was primarily a matter of numbers, tons of minerals, and smelting, which did not interest the two ladies very much. They strove to be patient, thinking about less severe things.

What memories, again, for Madame Montgrabel! Anzin Power Station, one of the principal affairs of the Montgrabel Company after its great beginnings. The transportation crises with which there had so much difficulty in that period, until 1925, had caused broader minds to see a radical remedy. "To overcome the difficulties of transportation, let's get rid of transportation!" they had said to one another. It was a definitive solution, a very simple program, but laborious and arduous in its realization. Monsieur Montgrabel, along with many others, had set to work. Madame Montgrabel remembered those years well!

It was simply a matter of bringing all the coal-consuming industries into the mining regions, around the collieries, of making our coal-bearing regions as many factories. Thus, there would be no more cumbersome transportations, no more slow and difficult circulation of an immense quantity of railway-wagons or barges, and hence, economies of time, of materials, of costs of transportation and of manual labor, and enormous savings of money. Coal was consumed on the spot, almost at the pit-head, by thousands of factories; then, heat, energy and light were sent forth electrically, radiating everywhere, transported over the greatest distances and distributed for industrial, agricultural or domestic consumption.

It had been long and hard, the period of labor, of creation—or, rather, of resurrection, for our mines and our factory installations had been destroyed by the enemy, emptied of all materials in the course of the frightful war, systematically, to begin with, in order to suppress competition, and in the end by demented rage, when the ferocious beast was at bay, and it had been necessary to reestablish, remake and recommence everything

"Good, good, very good, go for the triphasic 1800-volt alternators," said Monsieur Montgrabel. "That's fine."

The press of a button, and abruptly, the apocalyptic vision disappeared, cutting of the continuous purr of the factory landscape. Anzin Power Station was no longer there, nor its chief engineer.

III. The New Frontier and the Sacred Forest

Monsieur Montgrabel had begun to build the fortune of his company immediately after the great torment, in the formidable worldwide movement of affairs that followed the universal upheaval. When the last flames of the war were extinct, the last embers stifled, the great labor began on the seething planet: a gigantic task that could not wait, and which demanded the effort and good will of everyone; a world to be reconstructed, nationalities and states to be reconstituted on new and more solid bases; the economic life of peoples to be reestablished; a better and definitive form to be given to old Europe and the entire world, pulverized and recast in the crucible of war, along with peoples, ideas, customs, commerce and industry, and life in general.

Monsieur Montgrabel was only a petty industrialist making his debut in the aftermath of the war: open-minded, ready for anything, adapting to all situations and all métiers, getting a grip on all difficulties in order to overcome them, not recoiling before any task, and always disposed to knead possibilities and impossibilities in order to extract something advantageous from them by dint of ingenuity. Peace furnished him with a field of action in which to employ his qualities of audacity and his enterprising mind. He was well set for a good departure in the economic offensive.

Audaciously, with two associates, one American and one Chinese, he took over a sector of the new frontier and set to work vigorously, the American partner supplying the machines, the diggers, the equipment and all manner of foremen, while the Asian furnished the manual labor. That new frontier, the great circumference of which followed all the undulations of the ground—hills, mountains, rivers and watercourses, whether the majestic Rhine or gracious rivulets scarcely named on the map—in a continuous line, doubled or tripled in places, sustained in places by forts and well-aligned redoubts, was his first great affair. An enormous labor too—but Montgrabel did not find his share sufficient and subcontracted other sectors. While constructing his new frontier, Monsieur Montgrabel rebuilt the murdered towns of his sector, and there was agreement in recognizing those cities as the most successful towns in the entire series.

At certain points, the works of the new frontier encountered those of the Sacred Forest. The Sacred Forest—a forest scarcely born but more venerable and holier than the most ancient forests, more so than the forested sanctuaries of Gaul could be in our eyes—is the great forest that covers with its young shade and its adolescent stands of trees the entire devastated line of the former front: a forest as a sinuous and undulating as that had been, between fifteen and third kilometers broad and

43

nearly five hundred kilometers long, from the Yser to the Vosges and the Rhine.

What was it then? A broad deserted area, pitted with holes and fissures, a frightful lunar landscape coved in rubble, an immense battlefield furrowed by trenches, collapsed tunnels and blocked dugouts, bristling with iron brushwood.

The hideous destruction had been such that the corpse of a humble house, or that of an old farm, scarcely consisted of a few scattered stones. The cadaver of the forest was perhaps even more tragic in appearance, extended over vast plains as if buried, with thousands of desperate arms emerging from the ground.

One day, when the works of the new frontier intersected those of the Sacred Forest, and Montgrabel was examining with interest the vales covered with new plantations, he was hailed by a man who was studying a set of plans and maps among groups of workers of very various races.

"Montgrabel, my dear comrade, I knew that I'd end up running into you in this direction! I've followed your endeavors, you've reached mine. You see here Asia, Africa, America and Oceania fraternally digging the soil of old Europe after haring plied the rifle with her..."

Montgrabel recognized Monsieur d'Hérouville, a former comrade.

"Why, it's you, d'Hérouville. What are you doing here, then?"

"Gardener of the Sacred Forest, my friend! I'm planting, sowing and transplanting. I've come to collaborate with Nature in order to treat and bandage the wounds that the war has inflicted on the soil of France, to direct, assist and hurry alone the work of benevolent Nature. Instead of letting a simple tapestry of meager brushwood gradually cover the frightful scars, we're going to cure our land, do our best to make it flourish, and cover it with a mantle of verdure that will become thicker and more beautiful with every passing year.

"You see, it's beginning to take shape. Apart from respected points particularly celebrated for their commemorative monuments—museums of the enemy's crimes and the allied glories—we're beginning no longer to rediscover the former front and its horrors. We're bringing an entirely religious ardor to the impulsion of our labor..."

"How much work there is for the entire country, in the devastated regions and the preserved provinces, as well as the works of the new frontier!"

"So," d'Hérouville went on, "I'm directing the establishment of the Sacred Forest. Before anything else, I'm trying to save that which can still be saved of our murdered woods, our poor beeches and oaks, healthy firs and birches, those that persist, which have a stubborn life beneath the bark. I'm dressing the wounds, caring for or amputating our old ravaged Argonne, reconstituting it..."

"What hard labor!"

"Yes—there's the soil and subsoil to be remade, to be ground up with considerable importations of vegetal earth. Towns from all the regions of France, and even elsewhere, are sending us that vegetal earth: Burgundian, Auvergnat, Provençal, Alsatian, Breton of Languedocian."

"The Sacred Forest is made, my friend!"

"Almost made. Now, the great woods, the dense leafy thickets, the somber covert succeed one another in profound masses, hilly and verdant."

The two friends—the man of the Frontier and the man of the Forest—saw one another again; the two families became linked. Monsieur d'Hérouville had a charming daughter, Suzanne, who grew up and increased in beauty along with the trees of his forest.

When the almost-parallel endeavors of the Frontier and the Forest were concluded, having furnished frequent opportunities for drawing closer together, they continued to meet up. Monsieur d'Hérouville, although occupied with other projects, supervised his dear forest; in the summer, every year, he came to one of its various regions and pitched his tent there. In reality, that "tent" was a collapsible house, an authentic villa, even provided with a annex, where Monsieur d'Hérouville was able to provide hospitality to a friend desirous of renewal.

Between business trips, Montgrabel made sudden appearances; he sometimes stayed for thirty-six hours— a long sojourn for a man overladen with occupations, summoned hither and yon, fifty or two hundred kilometers, by the important affairs of a big company that was getting considerable larger from day to day. But he sometimes left Madame Montgrabel there with one or two of her children, very glad to take a pleasant breather in the freshness of the woods, in the midst of their studies.

It was thus that Charles, the eldest of his sons, while still young, felt caught by the soft and dreamy eyes, cheerful temperament and all the graces of Suzanne, a pretty lily-of-the-valley budding in the shade of the young copses of the Sacred Forest.

While Monsieur d'Hérouville pursued his career as a great forester, Monsieur Montgrabel continued shifting earth. He participated in the digging of the great canal between Paris and the sea, studied, promised, demanded and neglected for such a long time. It had finally been decided to construct it: a river cutting upstream of Paris, a broad channel, the Seine rejoining the Channel near Dieppe; ships of all dimensions were now traveling through the lush Norman grasslands, crossing paths with the hydroplanes that descended from the sky in order to settle on the foamy water like huge birds in a bath.

The Montgrabel Company had interests in a host of large-scale enterprises: electricity generating stations, airlines, terrestrial tubes for passengers or merchandise, companies importing produce from the colonies...

Then too, while European or American prospectors were roaming the countryside in order to discover riches in the subsoil, people thought about the soil itself, and the renaissance and development was seen a marked movement in the return of agriculture. In agronomy, the old systems were overturned by unexpected applications of new science. It was high time that those "new sciences" came to the aid of the good goddess Ceres, who was a little too backward, no longer able to succeed in nourishing all her children with methods dating from the emergence from the terrestrial paradise.

Today, electricity is the great slave, the universal workhorse, which human beings put to all tasks. They demand therefrom the most improbable services, the rudest and hardest labor, titanic efforts and the most minute and delicate operations. Obey, slave! Power the giant pile-drivers and the slender needles transpiercing mountains. They also say to it: "Make the wheat and vegetables grow, warm the blood of our vines, make the peas and potatoes prosper!" And electricity obeys.

Look at our countryside planted with tall stakes bearing bizarre accessories, covered by an immense and inordinately complex network of wires, comprising an interminable spider-web. That network is alimented by superpowerful electric machines, pouring their effluvia into the ground in order to stimulate the chemical operations underneath, and to obtain from our globe, which was said to be exhausted, crops worthy of the land of Canaan.

The peasants strive to keep up, abandoning the ancient routines; the schools of agronomy furnish engineers and foremen. But that is insufficient. Powerful associations have been formed to organize that cultivation over vast extents, constructing model farms for rational exploitation; companies of workers pass from domain to domain with their machines, following a studied circulation.

"My company also requires an agronomical branch," Monsieur said, as if in jest. "In my organization too, people must involve themselves with cereals, wines, oils, etc."

And, advised by Monsieur d'Hérouville, he turned his sight in that direction too. He soon had strong interests in the phosphate mines of Algeria, and also sent prospectors in search of deposits in Morocco. Two of his sons were at the Centrale with one of Monsieur d'Hérouville's sons; the third went to the École Supérieure d'Agronomie, and they all pursued studies brilliantly that would enable them to take leading roles in the general staff of the great Montgrabel Company.

One day, Charles Montgrabel, who had just left the Centrale among the leading members of his class, went to join the d'Hérouville family in their collapsible house in one of the most picturesque areas of the Sacred Forest, in the Argonne. He arrived alone by aircycle in order to surprise his friends, desirous of talking to them about his hopes and ambitions, and especially glad to see Suzanne d'Hérouville.

Monsieur d'Hérouville was no fan of present modes of locomotion. That man of the woods, determinedly rural, retained his sympathies for the old and most backward means of transportation; he went as far as the flying car, but, although a progressive man in other ways, he preferred to the fastest and most reliable airplane, the ancient horse, or at least the motorcycle and sidecar.

As Charles was parking his aircycle under the hangar, he saw Monsieur d'Hérouville and his daughter Suzanne arriving from a path through the wood. Exclamations were uttered, embraces exchanged. Charles was very happy; it seemed to him that on recognizing the number of the airplane, Suzanne had blushed with pleasure.

"Well, champion, are you content?" Monsieur d'Hérouville. "To graduate fourth in your class is very good."

"You know already?"

"I saw your father yesterday, by tele. We had a long chat. My compliments, dear boy! And I'm delighted by your arrival, delighted. We'll have some fine excursions together, you'll catch our breath under my trees, and we'll chat, especially about the Centrale, with Suzanne. We have a great deal to talks about regarding the Centrale.

"Why is that? Why that in particular?"

"Because, my friend it's time for her to think about a career; Suzanne has made very suitable studies at school, her scientific preparation is good. we're going to aim her toward the Centrale, and we expect that, with determination and perseverance, she'll be able to apply next year."

"Oh," said Charles, with a desolate expression.

"Eh! What? What makes you take that downbeat tone? Does our determination surprise you? You don't think she stands a good chance of being accepted? You have such a poor opinion to her brilliant faculties?"

"No, no! What annoys me, on the contrary, is that she'll be entering..."

"Yes, she'll be entering."

"And I've just left. I regret that she didn't decide on the Centrale sooner."

"Yes, at the age of twelve, eh?"

"Oh, that's true. I'm being stupid. It's me who's leaving too soon, let's say no more about it. In three or four years, Suzanne will be an E.C.P. engineer too..."

Suzanne laughed. She did not show any marked enthusiasm for the Centrale, but after all, it was necessary to embark on some career.

She set to work without showing an excessive ardor or a very great confidence when she applied. She was rejected twice by pitiless men who were not moved to make concessions by her slightly troubled gaze. O sorrow! Scientific careers remained closed to her.

It was necessary to go console her in the collapsible house, to which Charles hastened in order to offer his condolences.

And it was then that Charles, already launched in his father's great enterprises and in the research of the red coal, confessed to Suzanne's parents and his own, that he was in love...

Suzanne and Charles have now been married for six years and they have two charming children: young Gustave and Pierrette with the blonde curls. Their life is sweet for, in the course of his travels to the four corners of the world, Charles never fails to devote a part of his evenings to his family, thanks to a wireless tele apparatus that he transports into the depths of the most deserted wilderness.

Monsieur Montgrabel tried, in the early days, to stimulate his daughter-in-law to some utilization of her intelligence adapted to her tastes and aptitudes. But were Suzanne's aptitudes discernible? He studied her seriously with a gaze so clairvoyant in business matters, but a trifle distracted in other matters.

"My dear child," he said to her, "what if you were to study law? That wouldn't be bad; there'd be a position for you in the litigation section of the Montgrabel organization...an agreeable distraction and a useful occupation..."

Suzanne had therefore, commenced studies in law, again without enthusiasm. The spark was not there. The lessons in law lapsed and her husband, looking at here notebooks in order to tease her, found a good dozens little poems there distributed between a few lines of prose, under strange titles:

On synallagmatic and unilateral contracts

O songs of the stream hidden beneath the branches!
Souls of the leafy woods, fresh and discreet murmur!

The regime of privileges and mortgages

Calm down, my soul. The breath of the breeze
And the joyful sun
Dissipates vain dreams...

"Is Suzanne getting stuck into the law?" Monsieur Montgrabel asked his son. "Perhaps I'm mistaken, but it seems to me...

"Law? But she's abandoned it. Civil or commercial, it's too arid for her dreamy nature. She's begun to study high finance, which permits flights of fancy..."

"Too many flights of fancy! It's a good idea, all the same..."

"Yes, but I think that it's still beyond her aptitudes."

"Damn! That's already quite a few ineptitudes to her account."

Charles laughed quietly. He had just discovered in his wife's notebooks, it sonnets this time, but a little social and pastoral romance. An idyll between a Californian technologist and a young Picard woman—an idyll punctuated by considerations of the new situation of the semi-agricultural and semi-industrial populations of our modern rural regions.

That was, therefore, how she employed her time, to console herself for her numbers. Charles did not reproach his wife; he thought that she was fine as she was. Like the indulgent husband of old, he limited himself to joking about her lack of seriousness and allowed her to divided her time between her literary distractions and a small collaboration in Madame Montgrabel's social projects.

IV. A Family Dinner at the Montgrabel House. The Only Futile Person in the Household

Annette having talked, there was much discussion in the Montgrabel house about the famous lost handbag. Madame Charles Montgrabel went out every day, mysteriously taking air-taxis instead of going out in one of the house miniplanes.

What did it signify? What important objects could the lost handbag contain? What secrets had the wind carried away with it into the air? And poor Monsieur Charles was still out there in Java, suspecting nothing, even though he sometimes called his wife on the tele during the day, uselessly, Madame having gone out to search!

Monsieur Montgrabel senior manifested some surprise at these excursions, but he was so busy that such things soon slipped his mind. The conclusion of the staff, and Annette in particular, was that it was high time that Monsieur Charles came back and cleared up the mystery.

Instead of simply telephoning, Suzanne had gone in person again to the Central Lost Property Office, after having also enquired at the smaller Neuilly office.

Nothing. There was not the slightest trace of the modest red velvet handbag with the steel clasp, which Suzanne seemed to hold in such particular esteem.

"What's in it then?" one employee had the indiscretion to ask, irritated by her persistence. "Bank notes or love letters?"

Suzanne ran away, more worried than ever, and went along the bank of the Seine on foot, in the region that the airtaxi must have been flying over a few days earlier.

Young men from a nearby school manning hydroplanes were amusing themselves by performing stunts over the river.

"Be careful! Look out!"

That was addressed to Suzanne, who was getting too close to the edge.

Abandoning her search, she went back up quickly and headed for the air-station at the Pont de Neuilly in order to get an air-taxi. She risked it. The sky was calm; there was no wind and not even the usual traffic above the elegant quarter and the shade of the Bois de Boulogne, for it was a day of air races and the time when airplanes and miniplanes were taking off from the terrace of Saint Germain for the race from Saint-Germain to Brest and back, a sporting solemnity similar to the old classic horse races.

In the distance, toward the blue-tinted hills, above the innumerable villas scattered in parks and gardens, above the plains from which industry had fled, taking its factory chimneys to specialized regions, above Mont Valérien and all the villages that had become cheerful and florid again, the bright wings of airplanes could be seen from the Neuilly station, standing out against the verdure of the forests, and flocks of white airplanes taking off in groups at three-minute intervals in the direction of Brittany.

Suzanne returned to the Montgrabel house pensively. As she landed on the flight terrace, a large aircraft appeared through the first clouds, veering in an expert curve. Suzanne had no need to raise her head to recognize the particular purr of her father-in-law's airplane. She waited on the platform. Monsieur Montgrabel got down with his son Maurice and a gentleman with an important appearance.

"My daughter-in-law, Madame Charles Montgrabel," said her father-in-law to the gentleman. "Bonjour, Suzette! Dear child, may I introduce my friend Monsieur Larose, a former député..."

"Madame," said Monsieur Larose bowing.

"...Whose seat a lady, Madame...Madame...I can't remember, an advocate from Montpellier, has just stolen. Monsieur Larose is going to become my collaborator, I hope. Come in my dear friend."

Monsieur Montgrabel pushed Monsieur Larose into the left-hand elevator, descending toward his study, while Suzanne and her brother-in-law took the right-hand one in order to reach Madame Montgrabel's office.

"What does that gentleman do?" asked Suzanne.

"You heard—Monsieur Larose is a fairly well-known politician. My father told me in a low voice, while nudging me with his elbow: 'My future secretary, very probably.' I'm not entirely sure what he meant by that. My father has been rather mysterious for some

55

time. He's preparing something. What? We'll soon see...
Bonjour, Maman! You look superb today!"

"No," said Madame Montgrabel. I'm always exhausted..."

Madame Montgrabel was not alone in the little office annexed to the large office. There were three ladies with her—two of her daughters, Marcelle and Laurence, and a cousin, Madame Okonna—reclining in sumptuous Second Empire armchairs.

The cousin had just returned from a three-week trip to Japan with her husband, an attaché at the Japanese embassy in Paris, in charge of commercial affairs.

"And shall we see Cousin Okonna soon?" asked Maurice Montgrabel.

"Certainly," relied Madame Okonna. "This very evening. He's very busy at the embassy, you understand. Affairs in progress to regulate, and an entirely new question of aratory machines—electric, natural—created by one of our most famous engineers."

"Good!" sad Maurice Montgrabel. We have our mechanical construction establishments too. Competition in the family, then?"

The two sisters-in-law, Marcelle and Laurence, started laughing.

"And what about us? You don't know what Marcelle has just told me?" said Laurence.

"You don't know what Laurence has just told me?" said Marcelle.

Further laughter burst forth. Madame Montgrabel laughed too,

"Well," said Marcelle, "great news, we're all overjoyed. We've succeeded with the synthetic sheep."

"Well, Laurence continued, "we have in manufacture, in Australia, three thousand genuine sheep, alive, with authentic flesh, real legs of mutton, good cutlets, and wool into the bargain, while your synthetic sheep, my dear Marcelle, has no wool at all; it will never furnish enough to stuff a little mattress, your synthetic sheep in pill form!"

Suzanne gazed at her two sisters-in-law with such a expression of astonishment and incomprehension that they pretended to be scandalized.

"I observe with chagrin that Suzanne doesn't understand," said Marcelle, with great seriousness. "She still remains the futile person of the family. It's deplorable!"

"But what is the synthetic sheep?"

"The other?" said Laurence. "The true sheep, you must know that one? Yes? Well, Marcelle's synthetic sheep is in disloyal competition with the true sheep! O modern chemistry, yet another of your infamies!"

As tea, sweets and little cakes were brought in, the laughter ceased momentarily.

"Our beautiful our magnificent sheep," Laurence went on. "Nothing can compare with that. We manufacture sheep to refrigerate, magnificent, I tell you, because we have self-respect, my husband and I. They're superb! Last month, my husband took me to see them in Australia, three hundred kilometers from Sydney. Job's traveling. I spent four days with our sheep, flocks of twenty thousand, groomed bathed, shorn and pampered. It's admirable! Oh, Suzanne, you who rhyme neatly, sing about them, those lambs, bounding frolicking and growing fat..."

"All the way to the fridge!" said Edouard Montgrabel.

"And Marcelle thinks she can compete with us with her synthetic sheep! Get away! We'll fight, my dear, we'll manufacture so many real legs of mutton that no one will give a thought to your synthetic mutton beans. Oh, chemistry!"

"A captivating and beneficent science!" Marcelle protested. "Anyway, wait for our syntheses before pronouncing. Isn't that right, Suzanne?"

Suzanne was thinking about something else— doubtless the accursed lost handbag.

That evening, Monsieur Montgrabel only bought seven or eight people to the family dinner, among whom were the ex-député Larose; Monsieur Maklakof, a Russian associate, Madame Birchfield, the director of a large Anglo-French bank, Mercantile Union; a great aristocrat from the depths of India, the Maharajah of Pandjajabad; and Monsieur Galibert, the director of the telephono-cinematographic newspaper *Le Flambeau*, which appeared five times a day, in the morning, at noon, at six p.m., eight p.m. and eleven p.m.

During the meal, Monsieur Galibert remaining in connection with his editorial office—people still say "editorial" although the cinematic photographic component now takes a preponderant part in all periodicals— had the printer of the eleven p.m. edition on the tele, and sometimes that following morning's printer as well.

Monsieur Galibert caused interesting things to pass over the screen, scenes captured by adventurous reporters: the repression of a Turkish revolt in Asia Minor and troubles in one of the petty communist republics of southern Russia. Beautiful speeches were heard—in Russian, of course.

From time to time, when *Le Flambeau*'s articles threatened to inhibit the conversation, Monsieur Galibert put the tele on mute. The images filing past, which one could watch with a distracted or interested eye, depending on circumstance, could not drown out the Japanese cousin witty remarks or the remarkable financial deductions of Madame Birchfield, who was discussing political economics, philosophy and feminism with Monsieur Montgrabel.

"Soon, there won't be any politics anywhere," said Madame Birchfield. "Here in France, since the adoption of the new electoral system based on corporate representation, professional groups, groups of the agricultural, working, commercial, intellectual and bourgeois classes, etc, with the study and discussion of interests by experts, pure—or, rather, impure—politics has been immediately diminished, and almost abolished..."

"Add to that, the Japanese cousin put in, "the feminine conquests, the female elector and her admissibility to all functions."

"Certainly, I've long been won to the cause of feminist demands, insofar as they're reasonable," said Montgrabel. "Don't you see in all my enterprises, not only numerous female employees but also women in eminent positions: female engineers, directors, administrators, etc.? Look, close at hand, at the wife of my son Edouard, a doctor of law and deputy head of general litigation. You can see that the feminist cause has always found a determined and active partisan in me. But let's not go too far! I'm a little anxious..."

"We're heading for an upheaval," said Monsieur Larose, "toward a veritable reversal of roles."

"There's a recently-published book that seems to me to be a sort of manifesto," said Maurice, "*The Household of the Nation*, by a Monsieur Camille Boissy, an unknown. Do you know this Camille Boissy, Monsieur Galibert? Is it a pseudonym?"

"I believe so," said Monsieur Galibert. "Various suppositions have been made. Hang on—I'll just ask our literary critics whether the secret has been penetrated..."

He got up to go to the tele. The film stopped in the middle of a riot in Tiflis, where the cameraman had just had his arm broken by a bullet. In place of the furious Tcherkesses around the correspondent, who was bandaging his wound, a fat clean-shaven man appeared: *Le Flambeau*'s critic, tranquilly rereading a page for the phono.

"Camille Boissy?" he said, when he was brought up to date. "Still unknown. In my opinion, he must be some old white-bearded philosopher governed by his housekeeper and quite content to be. The mystery is overexciting public curiosity. To try to obtain revelations regarding the identity of the author, we've inserted into *Le Flambeau* a series of supposed portraits as varied as possible. The mystery remains impenetrable, the author isn't owning up. I'm sticking to my old philosopher. There's been talk of a female socialite..."

"Put up those portraits again, please. It will amuse us momentarily."

"Yes, let's see them again, please," Suzanne requested. "They've been mentioned to me, but I haven't seen..."

Le Flambeau's critic disappeared from the screen, and was almost immediately replaced by a gigantic question mark alongside the noble head of an old man.

The venerable male head disappeared, immediately replaced by a woman with a triple chin over a replete bosom, a severe face with spectacles and her hair in a small chignon at the top of her head.

"Our investigation," the tele continued, "is continuing in spite of our lack of success, and we are still hoping that Camille Boissy, in whom we recognize a great value as a thinker and writer, will not want to persist in an anonymity that is causing his readers and admirers chagrin."

Monsieur Montgrabel was no longer listening. He was chatting with the Maharajah and trying to find words of consolation for the distress that feminist doctrines had brought to the aristocratic castes of India, particularly at the court of Pandjajabad.

V. Between Paris and Java. A Tiger Hunt

Java! Rocks charred almost red, rosy ground, from which hot radiations and vapors were emitted, traversed by rivers that seemed to be fuming in the sunlight, and a superabundance of violent verdure.

Charles Montgrabel has been in Java for two months, caught up by important technical studies. His life, during these voyages—far too frequent for his liking—has no lack of the unexpected, picturesque colors and even petty incidents, but he no longer finds the same pleasure in all that movement, unexpectedness and changes of horizon as he did before his marriage.

The best moment, for him, was the hour that he was able to devote every day to his family, via the tele—a very brief moment, one hour in twenty-four!

Suzanne, for her part, affirmed to him that it was also the sweetest moment of the day. His absence was almost abolished; she recovered the patience to await his return. But for some time, she had seemed distracted or nervous, and when the anxious Charles had spoken to his mother about Suzanne's apparent preoccupation, Madame Montgrabel had told him that she had perceived it herself, without being able to find a reason for the changes she had noticed in her daughter-in-law. Decidedly, it was time to go home.

Charles, in a white jacket, looks good in a colonial helmet; the climate has not affected him. He is sitting at a folding table, under the veranda of his collapsible house, buried in exuberant verdure, which projects fans or sprays of long green points in all directions.

Some way behind him the prow of a miniplane is visible, posed in a space cleared of all vegetation, and in the cockpit is the head of a man working on the engine.

Charles is impatient. He has been ringing for some time. Finally, the screen clears. Suzanne appears, in the white décor of her bedroom, with the two children, who come running, joy on their faces.

Suzanne has to hold them to prevent them from hurling themselves at the tele screen, at the risk of breaking the apparatus.

"Hold on," said Charles, "otherwise you won't see the little monkey that I'm bringing you soon."

"The little monkey! The little monkey!" the children cried, manifesting an even more excited joy at that news. "Right away! Bring it right away, Papa!"

"Imprudent!" said Suzanne. "You've spoken too soon. They won't give us a moment's peace..."

"Can't you hear the beating of my heart, my dear Suzanne?"

"No," Suzanne replied. "The tele is an imperfect instrument; but we can see you, the children and I. We're very well. And you?"

"Not bad. Anyway, I'm coming back. I won't be sorry to return. It seems to me that I'm being somewhat forgotten, in Paris..."

"Oh!"

"Yes—today, again, I've come to the tele three times, uselessly. Only the chambermaid..."

"Oh!" said Suzanne.

"My dear Suzanne, another two days and I'll be leaving Java! You can see, my pilot is inspecting the engine, in order to take me to Batavia, where the dirigible is waiting for me. After that, three days of travel, stopovers at Ceylon and Bombay, and then to Cairo, where I have someone to see. And then Paris! That's the program."

"What joy! In five or six days you'll be here!"

"And I'm sufficiently content with my voyage. The Japanese and Australian engineers have been charming; I've been able to study their installations at Merapi, and other volcanoes in Surabaya, which should furnish energy, light and heat to Australia. They've had to overcome enormous difficulties: the climate, the constitution of the soil, seismic shocks, distance, and wild forests where tigers roam."

"Tigers! Oh my God!"

"Don't worry. A tiger-hunt was organized for this very day. You'll see that—I filmed the entire hunt. When you've dined, shortly, I'll put the film on the tele. The children can stay, you won't have too much emotion—there was no danger. Three dozen tigers were troubling the construction yards, and it was decided to get rid of the importunate beasts. With the Japanese and

Australian engineers and a few guests invited from Batavia we assembled our miniplanes. At dawn, when the tigers, having returned from their nocturnal hunts, were sleeping peacefully, airplanes went to deposit a dinmaker on the rocks, in the middle of their lair—a formidable instrument specially made for such hunts, whose frightful music—oh, my ears!—can be heard for ten leagues around, at the same time as a few asphyxiating gas shells were fired, to force the wretched beats to come out, in case the concert proved insufficient. And there were our tigers, maddened and bewildered, surging from the thickets, bounding, mewling, coughing and sneezing, in the midst of a swarm of other animals no less frightful, including some rather fine snakes."

"Imprudent!" cried Suzanne, covering her eyes.

"Vine snakes?" said Pierrette, interested, drawing closer.

"Don't come any further, my dear Pierrette, you'll get hurt," said Charles Montgrabel. "Yes, tigers and snakes of every size. And we were all there, but twenty meters up in the air, calmly and peacefully, in our circle of miniplanes, above our companies of tigers, increasingly panicked. We had no difficulty in shooting them with explosive bullets. A matter of a quarter of an hour, and the entire area was cleared. The final score amounted to four families with their progeniture: fourteen young tigers, already fully grown, more than a dozen snakes, and small game. Then we had lunch on the terrain, in the middle of our victims. It was very cheerful. There were several ladies, wives of our Japanese and Australian colleagues. I should have brought you with me."

"Thanks," said Suzanne.

"And me too," said Pierrette.

"Yes, when you're a bit older. I called you this morning to invite you to watch the hunt, but you'd gone out again. The chambermaid told me that you'd gone to the Lost Property Office to ask for a handbag dropped from a plane, and that it was the sixth time you'd gone to the office. Why not limit yourself to telephoning?"

Suzanne blushed.

"It was very precious, then, that handbag? Your jewels, perhaps? It's not my letters since I have no need to write to tell you that it's very annoying to be so far away from all of you—particularly you, Madame!"

"No, no..." Suzanne, embarrassed, blushed ever redder. Her husband saw her confusion and started to laugh.

"Right! I've got it—some little manuscript? Catastrophe! Sonnets to the moon, lost! Have you thought of offering a reward?"

"Let's not talk about it anymore," said Suzanne swiftly. "Let's talk about your return instead."

"One more week, and we'll be reunited. In any case, my father called me to the tele briefly yesterday; he also asked me to hasten my return. He has certain projects that he wants to talk to me about."

"He claims to have a great need for repose; he wants to rid himself of the cares of direction, to quit the business, presently prosperous in all directions. The great Montgrabel Company will become, he says, Montgrabel Sons, Sons-in-law and Daughters-in law, successors..."

"That's right. He's summoning us to a council to make the decisions."

"And Mother is rather anxious. These aspirations to repose don't augur anything good for her. She thinks that Father is, on the contrary, hatching new projects and simply getting ready to direct his activity into something new."

"That's more than probable," said Charles, laughing. "He mentioned something to me very vaguely, nothing precise, and then changed the subject."

"It's Mother, most of all, who has need of repose."

"As soon as I get back we'll arrange everything, a nice rest cure in the country, by the sea or in the mountains, for all of you: for the children, a cruise in a villadirigible in the sea air, above the Atlantic. That sounds nice to me, and I'll be there. But here's Bizot, my pilot, asking for me to cast a last glance over the miniplane's engine."

In fact, the pilot had come forward; his voice was audible, a trifle faintly.

"If you'd like to check, Monsieur," he said, "the engine's drawing well, the carburetion is perfect."

"I'll go see," Charles replied. "We can take a few turns around the house."

In the tele, he was seen to plunge into the background and bend over the apparatus; the music of the engine was faintly perceptible in the bedroom, functioning out there in the other hemisphere on Javanese soil. The purr stopped, and Charles came back to his family.

"Everything's ready," he said. "Now I have to go to work. Let's kiss. Until tomorrow, Suzannette! And above all, no more distractions!"

A rain of kisses departed from the bedroom bound for Java, and Java did its best to respond in the tele.

Suzanne returned the children to the nursery, where they were obtaining, while playing, their first notions of foreign languages with Franco-Anglo-Italo-Spanish nursemaids, which an extraordinary international twitter in the nursery, a fantastic lingua franca, especially when

Marcelle's and Laurence's children and those of the Japanese cousin arrived, with Dutch, Russian, Swedish or Japanese nursemaids. It was a miniature Tower of Babel

It is true that the same Babelesque mixture was found among all the domestic staff, as well as in the forcibly internationalized offices, in accordance with the principle that it is quicker to consult an interpreter than a dictionary.

VI. Social Changes and Political Ameliorations.
The Secretarial Spokesman

Monsieur Montgrabel's study is immense! And it is also flanked by an annex to the right and one to the left, which gives it the appearance of a gallery illuminated by large arched bay windows. The entire wing of the house occupied by the offices is a construction in reinforced concrete, iron and artificial granite, intelligently employed. Sacrifice has been made to old methods of construction for the habitation proper, linked to the office section, above the first floor, by walkways.

In the center of the building, the large flying platform looms up, rising to forty meters. Another flight-pad, less decorative, only rises up thirty-some meters, on the business side, for the coming and goings of the offices. That is certainly the more animated; planes are always circling it like a flock of birds seeking to alight, and the music of engines is a perpetual hum.

It is a little ministry, that Montgrabel house. All the numerous affairs and enterprises of the firm necessitate a general staff of directors, agents, engineers and technicians of every sort, a considerable number of male and female employees, as many of the latter in senior posts as in the minor personnel.

A large garden frames those buildings with its opulent shade and florid clumps. Madame Montgrabel, who retains old-fashioned tastes, has obtained in a sheltered corner of that garden, with some difficulty, a secluded corner where she grows flowers, when her affairs permit, and where she plays with her grandchildren: Pierrette and Gustave, the children of her eldest son, and those of her other sons, all still babies, who are not yet interested in the aircraft flying over the quarter and prefer the frolics of chickens—for, in a sumptuous chicken-run that qualifies as an aviary, Madame Montgrabel breeds chickens: simple hens that lay very ordinary eggs in their beautiful apartments.

From the high central flight-pad, above the tall trees hiding that aviary and Madame Montgrabel's rustic weaknesses, one overlooks the entire Parisian region, the quarters of wealth and luxury, which form a kind of new city from the Champs-Élysées to Saint-Cloud and Rueil, similar in places to an immense park with beautiful undulations of verdure, dotted with the white and pink masses of pavilions, turrets, cupolas and terraces of ultra-refined mansions. Closer than the ancient quarters, on the contrary, there are islets of foliage lost in the midst of opulent architectures born after the great worldwide quakes, the most formidable that the planet has suffered in the course of the centuries, when all the beneficiaries of the enormous tidal wave of wealth-displacement that resulted therefrom—a golden flood for some, breakage and shipwreck for others, for the many who could only save poor flotsam—the newly rich of all classes wanted to stabilize and install their fortunes in sumptuous frames worthy of them.

Looking a little more closely, one can perceive that certain houses, excessively ostentations in style, with overweening splendors, denote the exotic origins of the conquistadors and their builders: Patagonia or the depths of Ménilmontant. The excuse is that they were in a hurry. The peevish, in the early days, called it the "profitist" style.

From the height of the Montgrabel flight-pad, one can also see something like a large and wide green circle turning to the right and left of the Napoleonic triumphal arch, around old Paris. That is the park of the Bastions of '70, the former ramparts, replaced by a continuous line of gardens, lawns and sports-fields, which, distributing oxygen and life everywhere, has constituted nests of verdure among the massive blocks of old houses, and given birth to new quarters of joyful aspect all around the perimeter of the business center of Paris.

Monsieur Montgrabel has never had much time to admire the panorama that is displayed beneath the windows of his study; a distracted glance, cast in passing before each of the windows is almost all he can grant to the landscape—but that suffices to refresh his eyes and cause a reparative a vivifying beneath to pass into his

71

soul. After that, he feels that his mind is more alert, ready to receive the quotidian assault of preoccupations valiantly.

Today, before sitting down at his huge desk, as vast several billiard-tables set side by side, and covered with maps, drawings and files with cardboard covers of every color arranged in admirable order, Monsieur Montgrabel permitted himself a leisurely stroll past all the glazed bays, including those of the two annexes.

He rubbed his hands, and his face took on an increasingly marked expression of satisfaction. As he came to take his place in his armchair, he clapped his two sons, Edouard and Maurice, on the shoulder, and kissed his daughters Laurence and Marcelle, who were all waiting for him.

"Well," he said, "here we are united in grand council to discuss our little business matter. I've told you about my plans."

"No, Father, you've only dropped hints."

"Retirement, quite simply. I've been thinking about it for some time. Today, it's definitive, and you're taking over."

"Yes, we know that. But Charles isn't here. Is he up to date?"

"Yes, yes, like you. He's almost finished in Java and will be here in a week. Anyway we'll see him, I've warned him and I'm expecting him on the tele any minute... So, for me, it's retirement!"

Monsieur Montgrabel extended himself in his armchair and stretched his arms.

"I'm passing all the businesses over to you: all the work, the factories, enterprises, mines, blast furnaces, etc., etc. The entire organization, which was beginning to weigh upon my shoulders. A big deal—but I'll remain as an adviser, of course. I'm stepping down, but I'll always be here, if you need any advice, for, after all, you're young. I congratulate you, fortunate fellows! You seem young, at least for such vast responsibilities, even though there are several of you: you three, plus my sons-in-law, my daughters and my daughters-in-law, yes, all serious women. There's also Suzanne, still a little old-style, but I think that the social relations can be reserved for her. Don't blush, Suzette, it's not your fault, it's some frivolous grandmother from the time of basket skirts and romances, reappearing in you. Carry on the tradition, then! Marcelle prefers the laboratory to the drawing room, Laurence is too busy. They won't dispute those attributions with you..."

In fact, Monsieur Montgrabel's two sons scarcely seem to have passed thirty, like Charles, their elder. They are fathers: Edouard has three children, Maurice two. That is because people marry early nowadays, at an age when the men of old were still far from giving marriage a thought. Excessively prolonged bachelorhood is greatly frowned upon nowadays: a fortunate and salutary change, of considerable social range. Marriage is a departure, not an arrival.

As soon as a young man glimpses the paths open before him, he thinks about marriage, without demanding, in advance and above all, a dowry and an establishment. The dowry is no longer the primordial and determining factor that causes his heart to beat faster, for he has accepted the modesty of his beginnings in advance.

To embark thus, to venture together in the flush of youth, well equipped with courage and good will, on the river of life, without demanding a luxury cabin immediately, seems entirely natural now, after the great ruination and the great recommencement. People have faith in the future, and the future responds to that confidence

"You're taking over the direction, as we've said," Monsieur Montgrabel went on, "and now I'm free to savor the repose to which I've aspired for such a long time, in tranquility. You know as well as I do that all the company business is progressing well; disengaged from all preoccupation, therefore. I can devote myself entirely to my new plan, the little personal project that I've allowed you to glimpse."

"A trifle vaguely," said Edouard and Maurice, at the same time.

"Right—that's what I was afraid of," said Madame Montgrabel. "There's a little project..."

"Don't worry, my love—a little occupation for my old age. I've been thinking about it for a long time, and waiting impatiently for the time to arrive... So, I'm retiring, and to distract myself a little—as you can imagine, I'm not going to spend my days playing dominoes—to give my life a little interest, I'm going into politics, becoming a statesman!"

Madame Montgrabel and Suzanne could not repress exclamations of surprise. The two sons, Edouard and Maurice, did not manifest any astonishment. They were prepared, and had doubtless had some indications of their father's intention. Charles Montgrabel had just appeared on the tele, after a discreet ring; he had heard too, and had not reacted any more than they had.

"Yes, a statesman," Monsieur Montgrabel affirmed.

"Good! Very good!" said the two sons.

"Perfect," added Charles, in the tele.

Suzanne turned round abruptly. Between Monsieur Montgrabel's study in Paris and out there, in an unknown location beneath the banana trees of Java that scarcely possessed a name, the signs of handshakes and kisses were exchanged.

"Ah, you're there!" said Monsieur Montgrabel, turning to Charles. "Yes, everything's settled. I'm going into politics..."

"But there are no more politics today—you said as much the other day," objected Madame Montgrabel.

"There are almost none, but certain signs, like the exaggeration of feminist pretension...don't protest, Suzanne!"

"But I'm not protesting, Father."

"As I was saying, the exaggerations of feminism, which need to be combated. You've read that book, *The Household of the Nation*? Absurd utopias of which it's necessary to demonstrate the error and the danger. Women are electors and eligible—what more do they want? The direction of the 'household,' as the author, this Camille Boissy, puts it... And then, other exaggerations as well: 'Statism,' the tendency, no less utopian and unhealthy, to put everything in the hands of the State, to deliver all monopolies to it, and the direction of businesses. You can see perfectly well that there are still politics!"

"People thought that murky, troublesome and divisive party politics had been reduced to a tolerable minimum, "Edouard said, "with the new electoral regime, corporate representation and a large reduction in the number of legislative seats. And in fact, that had seemed to bring together..."

"The electoral rights conferred on women," said Maurice, "which was only just, and which no one has any reason to regret, has changed the spirit of deliberative Assemblies. Of the two hundred seats in the Chamber, women have conquered fifty-four, and it's almost the same proportion in the Senate. Affairs aren't progressing any worse—on the contrary—and a few good laws have come out of the collaboration of female députés and senators."

"Very good!" said Laurence, laughing. She was qualified in law and gone to court several time on the company's behalf.

"But the feminist party, represented in the Chamber by eminent women, I admit, is becoming more demanding and more ambitious from day to day—it's the atmosphere of the Palais Bourbon that's responsible. It has acquired a taste for power since two or three ministerial portfolios have been conceded to it, and it's making demands. That's the politics that is reappearing. Everything indicates it, damn it! Politics, with its struggles, its compromises, the bad politics of trouble and agitation, empty and harmful. Well, we'll struggle against it for a politics of reason, a politics of economic development. I shall struggle, I shall distract myself, I shall be a député..."

"A député!" cried Madame Montgrabel. "But you've always said that you didn't like palaver. A man of action before all, you were scornful of speech-makers and speeches. You even said that simple prudence required restricting the tongue of children who seem to hang too much on it, at any early stage, in order to prevent them doing any harm."

"I still think so! But have I said that I'm going to try my eloquence at the tribune? Another fortunate reform of our representative system has permitted men of action, businesslike députés who don't feel any oratory itch, to intervene. To put their word in, to give weight to their arguments in debates..."

"Oh, yes! The secretarial spokesman," said Charles, in the tele.

"Certainly! It's admitted, since the last elections, by the regulations on the Chamber: députés who mistrust their eloquence have a right to a secretarial spokesman. Thanks to that new institution, former parliamentarians, political men eliminated by universal suffrage, have returned to the Chamber as secretaries..."

"Of their successors!" said Edouard, laughing.

"Sometimes, exactly! It's all arranged; in six months I'll be in the Chamber. I've been making quiet preparations for some time, while occupying myself with my business affairs; I've anticipated everything. As for the reforms about which I ought to have thought, and which don't come to mind for the moment, to the various more or less important affairs to which I intend to devote my legislative activity, with the great experience of men and things that I've been able to acquire, and of which I shall allow my country to take advantage, well, we shall see. I'll think about that in the course of my leisure. Of course, not having a taste for palaver, I've already assured myself of a secretarial spokesman who will debate for me on themes I've prepared..."

"Who's that?"

"An advocate a former politician, former député, very talented...but you know him, he dined here the other day..."

"Monsieur Larose?"

"The same; he's accepted, in principle. We only have a few last details to sort out, and we'll sign the contract. He'll be here shortly—I don't like to let things drag on..."

Suzanne and her husband were no longer listening; they were chatting and arranging to meet at Bourges when the dirigible from India arrived.

Madame Montgrabel had calmed down. Since there was no big business deal lurking under the rock, as she had feared, they were finally going to be tranquil and able to savior weeks of true repose together.

*VII. Feminism and Statism.
M. Montgrabel and M. Larose, former député,
prepare to clash*

Monsieur Montgrabel did not linger over the development of his plans, and his sons asked no more of him than that. They knew that from the moment that their father had made a decision, it was definitive and that it was vain to seek objections. Montgrabel and his sons had resumed discussing important affairs in progress—the last works on the adaptation of the Puy de Dome, superphosphates, synthetic factories, the production of sheep in Australia—when Monsieur Larose the former député, was announced.

The visit was expected; Edouard and Maurice withdrew.

Without wasting any time, the two politicians got down to business. It was a matter of ascertained whether they were in accord on matters of principle before concluding the proposed arrangement. Among the social problems on which it was necessary to reach agreement, Statism and Feminism were in the first rank.

Monsieur Montgrabel got carried away. He perceived that he was not lacking in eloquence on occasion, and he was doubtless not sorry to demonstrate that to his future spokesman.

"So, this is what they want in the Statist party, still a small minority, but whose growth it would be imprudent to allow; this is what threatens us: everything to the State, monopolies of all sorts that they're trying to create every day, the most various and the least justified; the Industrial State, the State the great boss of everyone, taking charge of everything, and it will end up, won't it, manufacturing everything, selling everything, abolishing the most incontestable rights of the citizen, suppressing all initiative! Statism—which is to say, the worst form of socialism, insinuating itself slyly and transforming the governmental machine created with such difficulty by the experience of centuries…a monstrous aberration, a gross folly…"

Monsieur Montgrabel started pacing back and forth in his study.

A remarkable, open-minded man, that Monsieur Larose; he was lucky to be able to recruit him.

"My dear Larose," said Monsieur Montgrabel, clapping the former député on the shoulder, "I have an idea that we'll do great things together."

And they started to chat while walking, Larose taking notes.

"Ah!"" said Montgrabel, after a few minutes, "There's only the question of Feminism left."

"Oh," as to that," said Larose, "it's quite simple. It seems that you've taken a position a long time ago, and were one of the first, within the feminist movement. In all your enterprises, access to all positions, including the most senior, is open to women as to men."

"Yes, of course, I've gone as far as common sense permitted me to go...but today..."

"Today, you've changed...like me?"

"I haven't changed, I've stayed where I am: an apostle of reasonable feminism; but as I told you the other day, I refuse to follow it as far as crazy theories, the absurd utopias about which we were talking..."

"However, let's not forget that it's necessary henceforth to take account of the female electorate. Oh, it's necessary to recognize that we've been very imprudent. From one concession to another, this is where we've arrived: soon, perhaps, male and female electors in open conflict."

"It's necessary to react."

"Let's react!"

Monsieur Montgrabel, rummaged through the papers on his desk. He ended up finding a book in the file of the social endeavors in his factories, which he brandished with an expression of great indignation.

"The pretentions of Feminism are very clear: they clearly intend to dispossess men of the superior direction, to take the helm away from them. Look, I have it here, this book, this dangerous manifesto that is causing so much noise: *The Household of the Nation*. A fine title, modest in appearance, but a modesty that covers, in reality, the most insupportable demands. This book is a fireship, a veritable fireship!"

"I've read it, and I'm in perfect agreement with you. A seductive, adroit argument, which infiltrates into the mind of the reader and leads him gently not to revolt too much against the ambitious conclusions..."

"Panfeminism, quite simply! To men, external affairs, the care of *producing* by means of labor in all its forms, and then of making fructify in the country, etc. etc. To women, as in every well-organized household, the *housekeeping*—which is to say, the internal politics of the household, the care of maintaining the prosperity acquired by labor, good order and economy—which is to say, the diction of finances, or the household account-books, etc., etc."

"Everything, in sum—for Monsieur Camille Boissy doesn't want to demand more!"

"Has anyone managed to discover who this Camille Boissy might be?"

"Almost," said the former député, mysteriously. "I have a few tips. It's not a man, it's a woman. That mystery also has a great deal to do with the success of the book, with the noise that it continues to make in all milieux..."

"Say the scandal!"

"A movement is taking form. Camille Boissy's idea is attracting adherents almost everywhere, not only among feminist but among male electors. I have it from a reliable source that the advanced party of the intellectual section of the electoral body—universities, liberal professions—of the Parisian region is offering her a candidature in the elections. Same advanced intellectual section in the Marseille region, similarly..."

"Pooh! These intellectuals are so advanced they're derailed. That's not serious."

"It's very serious! With a little skill, they'll drag along the bulk of the electorate. You'll see—the election is certain..."

"And people claim that there's no longer any politics, nothing but business, nothing but the government of interests!" cried Montgrabel. "On the contrary, we're entering a new political phase. It's a crisis, a veritable crisis!"

Montgrabel had resumed pacing back and forth in his study, agitatedly, when someone knocked lightly on the door.

"Come in!" he shouted.

It was Suzanne, who put her head round the door without daring to come in. "Pardon me, Father, but I've just come from the Lost Property Office, and I was told..."

"What! You've lost something else?"

"No, it's still the same thing, the handbag from the other day. I was told at the Office that it was returned to you more than a week ago..."

"Not at all! Never! Mo handbag. I regret..."

"However..."

"Wait, it's coming back to me...it was a week ago, yes, not a handbag but papers...a little roll of papers. I'd forgotten. Let's see—where could I have put it?"

Still holding Camille Boissy's book, Monsieur Montgrabel began searching amid the clutter on his desk..

"Let's look at these stacks of paper...ah! Here it is! No, it's not that packet. Verses, isn't it, futile child? A few sonnets carried away by the wind? We'll find them eventually."

Montgrabel unrolled a few pieces of paper and read:

The age-old role of woman in the hearth...from the time of the tribe to our days, as well as in all the great civilizations... The increasingly important attribu-tions...have gradually equipped her with a kind of in-stinct of calm direction...

"Give it to me, Father, I beg you. Those are the papers that I lost..."

"Wait a minute—you're mistaken. What's this? *Two chapters to intercalate in the next edition.., of 'The Household of the Nation'*...but this isn't yours?"

"Yes, yes...no...yes! Give them to me, I beg you, and I'll leave you...forgive me for having disturbed you...but there were letters...a packet of letters..."

"Letters? From Charles? But no, he doesn't rote, he prefers the tele...your letters, then?"

"No, no!"

"Then whose? Yes, it seems to me that I've seen some petty papers, letters...I but I can't find them. What's the meaning of this, my dear child? Why this emotion? But Suzanne, what's wrong with my eyes? This is your handwriting...but in that case..."

"No, no, Father, give it to me, I beg you."

"But yes, but yes! It's definitely our handwriting, this...so...and this note signed Camille Boissy, also in your handwriting...what connection is there between this Camille Boissy and you?"

"This Camille Boissy?" said Larose, very interested, his eyes lighting up.

"No, it's not possible! What, you, my little Suzanne, the author of that famous book...absurd and false, of course...but so seriously thought, established. It's you who amuse yourself writing these things, I repeat, of violent absurdity...and so pernicious...!"

Suzanne had collapsed into her father-in-law's armchair, like a criminal, lowering her head, looking up at Monsieur Montgrabel, who continued, with the most culpable indiscretion, to leaf through the papers and pick our phrases, which he read, affecting a fearful surprise.

"You go far, my little Suzanne, my dear Monsieur Camille Boissy. Your *Household of the Nation* is a veritable manifesto—a manifesto of revolt and usurpation! That's the word: usurpation! Look—now you've take my armchair and my place at my desk. It's symbolic, that."

Suzanne leapt out of the armchair. She would have liked to run away, but she did not dare under the mocking eyes of Monsieur Larose.

"And I thought you were simply amusing yourself writing little poems or sugary romances for petty demoiselles!"

"Excuse me, Father, and pardon me. You're right, a thousand apologies…I don't know what got into me. I'll go and burn all this immediately."

As she disappeared, former député Larose began to laugh.

"My dear friend," said Montgrabel, "this might make a disagreeable little story. You're in the company now; you'll help me to stifle it…"

When the former député had gone, Montgrabel shrugged his shoulders again, and then started rummaging through the files on his desk, talking to himself in a low voice:

"You see that! That little Saint Touch-me-not who takes it upon herself…I'll have her reprimanded by her husband… However, yes, it seems to me that there was something other than those few sheets in the packet of papers that was brought to me…where could I have put it? What file has it slipped into…? Ah, here's something. Oh! But what's this?"

Monsieur Montgrabel had just discovered a little envelope under a pile of reports and, as he read the address, his terrible eyebrows suddenly furrowed:

CeBy
Poste Restante, Bureau 48, Montrouge

"CeBy—Camille   Boissy,   of   course.   Poste
Restante…that's more serious. The envelope is empty!
Suzanne! Suzanne! The only futile person in the family…and frivolous! Yes, but exactly how far can that frivolity go?"

Suzanne, emerging from her father-in-law's study
in great distress, bumped into her chambermaid, who
was looking for her.

"Madame, Monsieur is asking for Madame at the
tele…"

She strove to smile in order to dissimulate her emotion, and went to her apartment, rather slowly, in Annette's opinion.

Charles was waiting at the tele, his expression a trifle impatient. The overabundant vegetation of the Javanese forests on the flanks of volcanoes was no longer
visible behind him, but it was still Java. He was in a cabin   of   a   large   dirigible   of   the   Java-India-Paris-
Amsterdam-London line—a small but comfortable cabin
linked to the dirigible's wireless post.

"I thought you'd gone out again," said Charles.
"Always out. I was afraid of not seeing you before leaving Java, in order to reach an understanding. In half an
hour we'll be taking off from Batavia. I've finished everything here. I'm quite content with my voyage. It's going perfectly, with regard to the red coal. I'll be in Paris
n Saturday. Too many ports of call, four days of travel—
it's interminable. Anyway, I hope that on Saturday,
you'll come as far as Bourges, the last stop, to meet me.
A little excursion with the children!"

VIII. Meeting the Dirigible

"Who would have believed it?" said Monsieur Montgrabel, who had just brought the strange revelation to his wife—without, however, mentioning the strange envelope addressed to *CeBy, Poste Restante*. "Who would have supposed that such things could emerge from that light head, my love?"

"It's extraordinary," said Madame Montgrabel, still incredulous. "It's not possible!"

They had the confession of the guilty party, however; it was necessary to yield to it. Monsieur Montgrabel remained involuntarily preoccupied, and sought in vain to know who could have put those singularly advanced ideas into his daughter-in-law's head.

And that envelope of the Poste Restante letter? It was necessary to proceed with a serious investigation. It's necessary to penetrate the Camille Boissy mystery. Come on...I'll find someone in my office to make discreet enquiries, some fine sleuth...

Unfortunately, a vague echo of the revelation had reached the press, for *Le Flambeau* was talking about its investigation again and had reiterated its question mark with new silhouettes, all female this time: a series of unknown women whose features were rendered with deliberate imprecision, some grotesque, others, on the contrary, very elegant. And *Le Flambeau* announced that the circle was closing in around the mysterious Boissy.

The searchers were becoming ardent, for Suzanne found in her post a small newssheet from Marseille, *La Femme Enchaînée*, the organ of the advanced party. Suzanne scanned the newspaper rapidly. As she feared, the name Boissy recurred on every page, with citations or developments of the ideas launched by the imprudent Boissy.

Time passes, in spite of all annoyances, and the great day of Charles Montgrabel's return has arrived. According to the latest wireless news, everything is going well aboard the dirigible *Himalaya*, which is completing its journey in ideal conditions.

News has come in, *en route*, from Ceylon, Bombay, Cairo and Marseille; the last port of call is Bourges. Charles allows a slight delay to be foreseen, however; instead of three p.m., the *Himalaya* is expected to touch down at Bourges between five and six p.m. As the *Himalaya* might catch up with its timetable during the morning, however, Suzanne has made her preparations to depart early at about eleven a.m. in the miniplane, as he has requested.

It's much too soon, thought the pilot, *we're not in any hurry. It's a lovely day!*

The weather promises to be superb: a calm sky, no wind, not even a breeze, and the sun shining brightly. The pleasure will be complete in heading into the blue, through the pretty white clouds floating here and there, filing past in all tranquility, like well-drilled squadrons, toward the south-west.

Suzanne is very agitated, the children are having difficulty not jumping for joy. Fortunately, the miniplane is closed; it is a comfortable and very reliable apparatus, with a light turbine that consumes less fuel than the old internal combustion engine.

Nestling inside the vehicle, hugging her children in her arms, Suzanne is dreaming and not paying any attention to the route. They are going slowly, the pilot has no reason to hurry, and he is making a little tour first in order to take advantage of the fine weather.

"Where are we, then?" Suzanne asks, perceiving the tower of Gisors on its hill beneath her. "But that's the canal from Paris to the sea," she says, lowering the window slightly. "That's Gisors down below, and over there, it's the Seine that's glittering under the cliffs of Château-Gaillard."

"Yes, Madame," he pilot replies.

"That's not the route from Orléans to Bourges!"

"Not exactly. I've made a detour to fly under the little clouds. We have plenty of time; it'll be prettier and calmer for the children."

"We're going to miss the *Himalaya*, though!"

However, the miniplane, while flying at low speed, had already passed Bourges, and by some distance, when Suzanne's watch scarcely marked two p.m. The miniplane was describing large circles; the pilot, to occupy the time, headed eastwards in the direction of the Jura, but on perceiving the green ridges of the mountains and, further away, the white summits of the Alps, Suzanne became anxious again. The miniplane turned westwards again, more rapidly.

When they were in the vicinity of Moulins, on the route that the *Himalaya* ought to be following, Suzanne, reassured, told the pilot to find a good landing-ground. The children were beginning to become restless in the miniplane, they needed to stretch their legs, and it was necessary to let them have a snack.

A favorable spot was soon discovered, in a lovely meadow on the crest of a hill, from which they could keep watch on the entire horizon. The miniplane made a fine descent in a slow and gentle spiral; the children were about to jump down to the ground joyfully with their mother, when a man with a palette in one hand and a canvas in the other bounded fearfully from a bush, which hid an easel and a painter's parasol.

"Hey! Hey! One can't risk oneself in the country-side any longer, then, without being crushed?" cried the painter, furiously.

"No, no," replied the pilot, cheerfully. "Have no fear—don't move, stay where you are! I'd seen you...there's no danger. You can resume your place."

"How can one work like this always threatened, always on the point of receiving ships or people one one's head?" the painter grumbled—but Suzanne came to apologize and calm him down. He was an old man, between sixty-five and seventy, a man of the former regime, and his emotion could be forgiven

While the children had a snack on the grass, the old painter continued moaning, pacing back and forth, palette in hand. Suzanne looked at his canvas and lavished compliments on it in order to finish dissipating the ill humor of the landscapist disturbed while working. She uttered admitting exclamations and sought the means for slipping in an offer of purchase.

In any case, it truly wasn't bad, that little study: a simple clump of trees in the foreground, lovely tones of green in the vaporous distance.

They were soon chatting like good friends. Suzanne having told him that she was going to meet her husband, the painter approved; but when she had added that he was an engineer and traveled a great deal for large-scale projects, he pulled a face.

"Yes, yes, they're going to doom us and dislocate the entire planet, your husband and all the rest! Poor Alps! They've been excavated over and over again, pierce with holes like a Gruyère cheese. And tubes threading that granite Gruyère, and flight-pads, platforms and garages for airplanes everywhere, on my lovely old rocks, or at the very top in the snows, and skyscrapers in all directions, and streams dammed, and in between, under the eternal glaciers, exploitation mines for the white coal!"[5]

"It's all necessary," said Suzanne, mildly.

"They always say that!" The old painter was talking through his beard; Suzanne had difficulty hearing him very well. She turned back to his study in order to calm him down.

"Truly delightful, that landscape. And as it is, how..."

"No, I don't sell," he said, "it's for me. Ought I to tell you everything? You have an air about you that makes me sympathetic, and gives me confidence. Listen, I'll tell you, but quietly. Come closer. There...I'm quite well off now, I only work for myself. Well, I made my

---

[5] "White coal" was a phrase already used in 1919 to refer to hydroelectric power.

fortune…oh, it's difficult to say it…I daren't tell you, you'd be horrified…"

Suzanne looked at him fearfully, recoiling toward her two children.

IX. In the Dirigible from Java to Bourges and Paris.
An Old Cubist

The old painter was speaking more and more into his beard, as if to hide his words there, and the painful confession that emerged reluctantly.

"The thing is, in my youth, I was...don't be afraid, I won't bite, I no longer bite...I was...a cubist! You know, cubism: prismatic portrait and landscapes, fragments of people and things cut up into prisms, triangles, etc. I was one of them! You mustn't tell anyone—no one knows, I've changed my name. No one suspects—but I'm famous in the Rue Laffitte. Yes, it's in cubism that I earned my income. Oh, youth, youth! Now, I'm making up for it. Look at my study. Isn't it the case that one can't perceive it, that no one can any longer suspect it? Madame, I'm full of contrition, I'm overflowing with contrition! Listen carefully!"

Suzanne only heard half of the confidences of the repentant cubist. She interrupted him abruptly.

"Oh my God! I'm sorry, Monsieur, but I must go. I'll miss the dirigible!"

The pilot lifted up the children and placed them in the miniplane. Suzanne embarked thereafter. The old painter continued his protestations, at a respectful distance from the apparatus, but nothing at all could any longer be heard.

Thirty seconds later, the apparatus got under way, took off, veered gracefully away, and gained altitude. They returned in the direction of Bourges prudently, but they were not in as much of a hurry as Suzanne had pretended; it was necessary to tack for some time and describe circles in the blue and the clouds, descending and regaining altitude, going back and forth within a certain radius around the town before finally distinguishing, without fear of error, the imposing silhouette of the great dirigible *Himalaya*, emerging from a long streak of cumulus on the horizon and advancing majestically, casting a giant shadow on the ground below.

"There it is there it is! It's the *Himalaya*, children. Here comes your Papa. In a quarter of an hour, we'll see him!"

The pilot accelerated the engine in order to arrive at Bourges at the same time as the dirigible, the considerable mass of which Suzanne ant the children could see growing visibly by looking back.

"Quickly, quickly!" said Suzanne. "It's gaining. We'll never reach Bourges!"

"But we're there, Madame," said the pilot. "There's the cathedral directly below. I'm heading for the flight-pad now."

In fact, five hundred meters beneath the miniplane, glorious sunshine bathed the town, emphasizing the tall trees lining the cross-hatching of the streets.

In addition to the Gothic cathedral, other buildings loomed up, those of a frank modernism: the station of the Paris-Clermont-Barcelona tube, with its access platforms; and higher up, slimmer, the great aircraft flight-pad, an iron steeple, light and performated, surrounded by its globular beacon, bearing its luminous number like a plume in the first mists of the evening.

Suzanne did not take the time to admire it; she had turned back toward the dirigible, which was slowing down and maneuvering in order to land on the platform of the flight-pad. The elegant miniplane also swerved and seemed to glide through the air, describing a long curve that brought it closer to the *Himalaya*.

A great deal of movement could be distinguished on board, of passengers about to get off and going to the walkway, suitcases in hand; at the windows of the cabins, others were examining the landscape. At the very front, near the multimotive nacelle of the prow, someone was waving his arms broadly.

"Papa!" cried the children.

"Bonjour! Bonjour!" replied the man. "Land!"

The miniplane was already turning, overtook the dirigible, and went to land on the flight-pad on the opposite side, near two helicopters that had also come to meet the *Himalaya*. Charles Montgrabel had leapt down on to the terrace; he helped Suzanne and the children out of the miniplane himself.

"Come with me right away," said Charles, after the first tumultuous embraces. The *Himalaya* only has five minutes; we'll go back to Paris together; the miniplane can return to the house alone."

The dirigibles of the great Far Eastern lines are luxuriously fitted out. The passenger space is perhaps measured, but makes up for it in its installation. Between the front and rear cabins, in two rows, port and starboard, in the large lounge-dining room, decorated by Japanese artists. There, on comfortable banquettes, the hours of idleness pass quickly with a few books or magazines, or in the contemplation of the varied scenes that unfurl interminably down below: wild forests with giant trees, projecting their lianas and their bouquets of overabundant vegetation toward the violet depths that can be glimpsed from on high; plains of all colors, depending on the crops, improbably bright yellows, greens, browns and reds; rivers flowing broadly through those plains, and torrential streams descending in foaming cascades over rocks scorched by the flamboyance of the sun; and cities of magical architecture, set in emerald or coral...

Then there is the sea, blue, pink or mauve, in accordance with the hour, islands with ragged contours, isolated or strung out in long archipelagoes, rocks standing up in circles of foam, or volcanic islets, the smoke of which rises up toward the dirigible.

Thus, the time passes quickly on board, in the lounge or on the walkways. Nevertheless, Charles Montgrabel is overjoyed at the arrival. He has taken Suzanne and the children to his little cabin, and they are chatting. In half an hour the airship will be flying over Paris, and they will be home.

"Everything still going well *en route*?" asked Suzanne. "No hitches?"

"No, a perfect crossing, no incidents. I'm very glad to arrive. Far away from you, I worked hard in order to bring my return forward. I think I got a few good ideas, but I was in a hurry to get back. Yes, I was in haste. I've had enough of long absences. It's definitely bad or everyone. I've had enough of it!"

Charles' voice had changed completely. Suzanne and he looked at one another, and each of them thought that they discerned more anxiety than joy in the other's eyes.

"Come on," said Charles. "You seem worried...yes, worried. What's the matter?"

"No, no, I'm joyful. Just a little emotional..."

"But yes, something's wrong. What is it that isn't going well? There are no health problems, and the rest is secondary Tell me the rest, quickly!"

Suzanne remained mute for a moment. Finally, she decided.

"There is something, yes," she said, lowering her head. "It's me who...who...has to confess to you..."

"Something to confess to me!" Charles cried. "What? What is it?"

Suzanne still hesitated, her gaze lost in space, but the landscape filing past rapidly below reminded her that they would soon arrive in Paris. It was necessary to have said everything before disembarkation.

"Perhaps you've heard mention of a book that appeared a few months ago, *The Household of the Nation*..."

"Too much in recent days."

"That's unfortunate. If you knew that I..."

"But in sum, what is it?" cried Charles. "For a week, every time I've been summoned to the tele by Maman or my brothers, it always ends up being a question of this Camille Boissy. I've sensed something troubling in the ambiguities and the reticence...disturbing, even. What have I to do with this Camille Boissy? My father has also said something to me, in a constrained manner..."

Suzanne hid her face behind Pierrette's blonde curls.

"Come on, quickly, what is it? You know him, then?"

"Only too well, alas!"

"What?" Charles had stood up, red in the face,

"Yes, much too well. The author of that absurd book...is...forgive me, Charles...I...I'm guilty...in sum, Camille Boissy...is me!"

"Boissy is you? He's you?"

"It's me who wrote it, that book...and published it, alas!"

Charles looked at Suzanne for a long time. That saddened face, those eyes in which tears were pearling, stirred his heart. He drew the children on to his knees and strove to smile.

"Good, I've come back to sort all that out. If my father is discontented, there must be, in that inconvenient...masterpiece, something embarrassing for us. Is the real name of the audacious Camille Boissy known, then? Has the success of the explosive book intoxicated you, and you haven't been able to keep quiet? But is that really all? Everything?"

Again, his face darkened. The almost musical modulations of a siren interrupted him; they were arriving. Numerous footfalls could be heard in the walkways, shouts and whistle-blasts directing the maneuvers.

"The Eiffel Tower!" said the children.

"Paris!" said Charles. "Let's go! Let's not talk about it anymore. We'll see about it later!"

Very gently, with scarcely a slight quivering of the engines, the dirigible descended toward the great flight-pad of Issy-les-Moulineaux. There, in the middle of an immense landing-field, five enormous hangars could be seen, forming a circle, meeting at the center, at the base of the flight-pad, a little Eiffel Tower carrying the vast flight-pad at a height of five hundred meters.

There were eight great flight-pads like that for the important lines, distributed in favorable spots around Paris, and others were planned.

There was a great deal of movement around the flight-pad. Numerous aircraft of every sort were awaiting passengers on the second platform. A pleasure dirigible hired by some nabob of finance was swaying up above, ready to fly to Scotland for a hunting expedition. There was a great animation aboard, where the passengers were celebrating the departure noisily.

Down below, a huge freight-dirigible was projecting, outside its hangar a prow reminiscent of the head of some prehistoric monster quitting its cave in order to run at the multitude of Myrmidons, busy human ants swarming around it.

Having already arrived five minutes earlier, the miniplane was waiting on the platform to take its masters back to the house.

X. Jean-Marie Jézéquel, Submarine Shepherd.
The Good Idea

"Jean-Marie, I'm so glad!"

"Me too, Annette, but you've taken a long time to get through."

"Couldn't. A snag, I don't know what, in the apartment teles. Not working."

"We're taking on fuel at the Ouessant post, and I'm taking advantage of it. All going well? Good!"

"You look good Jean-Marie."

"You too, always lovelier. People dress well in Paris. People become elegant—that worries me."

"That's necessary, you know, Jean-Marie, at the Montgrabel house..."

"See you soon, Annette!"

"Patience, my poor Jean-Marie. You have a good wage..."

"And no opportunities to spend it at a depth of twenty-five or thirty-meters," Jean-Marie interrupted, laughing.

"So much the better in all respects. That will give us more savings for the marriage."

That conversation was taking place at the tele in Monsieur Montgrabel's study, to which Monsieur, coming in unexpectedly, was listening, his hand on the knob of the door, which stood ajar.

Monsieur Montgrabel seemed to be in a slightly bad mood, but nothing serious. During the three days since his son Charles had returned, life in the house had resumed its habitual course. Everything was working out quite well. Every evening, Monsieur Montgrabel conferred with his sons and settled with them all the questions relative to current business. The majority were so important that he could not see himself being free of all preoccupation and completely free in his movements for some time.

Madame Montgrabel was demanding that he keep his promise of a long period of complete vacation, and absolute rest cure. He had made a formal engagement, and it was necessary to keep his word without further delay. On the other hand, certain annoyances were threatening to become aggravated. There was still that unfortunate book of Suzanne's! The newspapers appeared to be on the right track; there had certainly been partial indiscretions regarding the identity of the author, for it now seemed universally admitted that Camille Boissy was a woman. Now, a quantity of magazines and pamphlets were arriving at the house every day, in which there was always some allusion to Camille Boissy.

After remaining at the door for two minutes, he opened it entirely and went in, just as Jean-Marie was saying: "Yes, Annette, it will be nice, then—the good life in Cézembre. Me occupied with administrative material, in order to come home cheerfully at noon and in the evening, to my wife, in our little house. I can already see us there…"

Annette uttered an exclamation which cut off the happy Jean-Mruire's speech.

"I beg your pardon, Monsieur," she said, turning round, slightly confused, toward Monsieur Montgrabel. "It's just that…"

"What?" said Monsieur Montgrabel.

"It's just that the teles in the house have broken down; only those in the office are working, and I was worried about my fiancé."

"Oh, that's your fiancé?" said Monsieur Montgrabel. "Don't run away."

"Yes, Monsieur, Jean-Marie Jézéquel of Saint-Malo. Like me…"

Jean-Marie, slightly nonplussed, had taken off his cap and was standing at attention in the tele.

"We're going to be married in eighteen months…"

"Yes, so I've heard. He looks like a good fellow, Jean-Marie Jézéquel, very nice. Don't run away. Tell me, where is he, at this moment? It's quite rugged, that rocky beach on the tele. Where is it?"

"Ouessant, Monsieur," Jean-Marie replied himself.

"Yes, not bad. A slightly rough sea, in spite of the good weather, a fine coast, very jagged, and solitary. What are you doing in Ouessant, fishing? You're a sail-or?"

"A submarine shepherd, Monsieur."

"What?"

"Excuse me—that's what we call ourselves, in jest. I belong to the administration of Submarine Agriculture and Fisheries, quartermaster aboard submersible number four."

"Ah!" said Monsieur Montgrabel. "I've heard mention of that. Yes, yes...the methodical exploitation studied by the ministry, the management of the sea-bed on the coasts and at sea, the organization of fisheries, husbandry and surveillance."

"Yes, Monsieur, the husbandry and surveillance of fish in the submarine pastures, the destruction of porpoises and other predatory species. That's why we're known as submarine shepherds."

"And you're comfortable aboard your submersible number four? Life isn't too hard?"

"We're very comfortable. We have more distractions than landlubbers or surface fishermen imagine. I wouldn't change places with a forester on land.

"Hang on!" said Monsieur Montgrabel. "That's an idea, yes, a good idea...!"

Leaving Annette slightly bewildered, and Jean-Marie still standing at attention, he quit his study and, without going into any of the offices, headed for his wife's apartment.

H found Madame Montgrabel very busy, arranging boxes, filing mountains of files and closing drawers.

"Excellent, my love!" he said. "You've finally began your preparations for moving. I've begun, it won't take long."

"And where are we going?" asked Madame Montgrabel, leaving her rearrangements.

"I propose a charming, delightful location, new for us, not too frequented. Various aspects, the picturesque and the unexpected, numerous distractions, fishing, even

103

hunting. Perfect calm, freshness. No hindrances. An ideal holiday location, in sum!"

"That will be excellent for Suzanne, very sad for Charles, who appears morose and tormented. It's necessary to elevate them from their chagrin," Madame Montgrabel replied. "Eventually, things will sort themselves out. Where is it, this ideal holiday location?"

"On the sea-bed."

"What?"

"I'm not joking. I'll explain…but wait a minute, while I see, before we rejoice, whether there isn't some snag…"

Monsieur Montgrabel ran into a drawing office to one side. The employees had gone to lunch, it was possible to talk freely at the tele.

He rang urgently.

"B.X.Z. 28-4? General Yachting Company… Yes, very good. Is that you, Monsieur Didier? All going well…? Yes, thanks. Tell me, I'd like to hire…"

"Like the other year, Monsieur, one of our big yachts?"

"No, a submersible this time. Do you have a good submersible yacht?"

"Yes, certainly, several, in fact…"

Behind her husband, Madame Montgrabel followed the conversation. She was beginning to understand. In the tele Monsieur Didier could be seen in the process of bringing out large, brightly-colored photographs from a box-file, representing boats of all categories: yachts, hydroplanes, airboats, submarines, etc.

"This is the best of our submarines," said Monsieur Didier, presenting a photograph. "The *Espadon*, an excellent vessel. I know nothing approaching it, even in America. Quite new, scarcely three years…first-class crew. Commandant Guénard has been sailing with the submarine fleet for ten years; he's a likeable man and very strong, full of resources..."

"Very good, very good! I'll take the *Espadon* for six weeks; notify him. Where s it moored?"

"Roscoff."

"Thank you; we'll be there tomorrow evening. Thank you, Monsieur Didier; I must run to make preparations."

"You don't need hydroplanes?"

"One or two, and I'll bring our aircottage. Thank you, and *au revoir*."

Monsieur Montgrabel turned round.

"Well, it's done," he said. "You heard? I've rented the *Espadon*. As I was certain of having your approval, I decided immediately, for fear of seeing the boat hired by people in a hurry..."

Madame Montgrabel reflected. Her husband started giving her an account of the explanations given to him a little while ago by Jean-Marie Jézéquel. It was necessary to have seen it! Monsieur Montgrabel reproached himself for not having thought sooner of a holiday in a submarine.

"With stations wherever we wish, ports of call when required, a pied-à-terre when the Breton or Norman bays tempt us. And if, by chance, I have a little trip to make to Paris, the miniplane will be there. Quickly, to the trunks and the packing. I'm in haste to find myself one...no, in...the *Espadon*."

Monsieur Montgrabel departed like a whirlwind, immediately summoning his chiefs of staff.

As he was about to go into his office he bumped into a young man in a corridor, who had just emerged from

the large elevator and was negotiating with the employees.

"Pardon me. I'm a reporter for *La Minute* and I've
been instructed to ask you what you think about the
questions raised by a recent book, *The Household of the
Nation*..."

Monsieur Montgrabel started, his eyebrows frowning.

"*The Household of the Nation*?" He said, in a furious tone. "Don't know it. Please excuse me...no time to
read...pleased to have met you..."

It was definitely necessary to leave as soon as possible. In five or six weeks the fuss around the exasperat-
ing volume would have calmed down, people would be
talking about something else. Charles would have the
time, during the vacation, to give Suzanne a good talking
to, to demonstrate her imprudence and make her return
to harmless poetry.

The best thing, Montgrabel thought, *would be to
find some worthy fellow who would declare himself to be
the author of the book. We'll see...we'll think about that
aboard the* Espadon. *To work!*

The following afternoon, the Brittany tube, always
crowded at that time of year, took the entire family away
by means of a seaside express. So comfortable, and entered so swiftly into habit, the electric tubes, substitute
for the old railways, now used primarily for merchandise, except for small local lines. They travel so marvelously. In two and a half or three hours, the express tube,
in spite of stopping in the big cities as well as the junc-
tion stations for the coast, deposits its passengers in
Brest.

Monsieur Montgrabel had a reserved compartment
screwed on to the end of the train. At quarter past six,

the family descended at Morlaix, where the miniplane was waiting at the station flight-pad to take everyone to Roscoff.

The weather being marvelous and the temperature mild, the flight was good. The sea was unfurling gently and lapping the rocks of the coast and the inlets of the Morlaix shore with roseate waves. Near Kérouzéré, in one of the prettiest inlets of fine sand, framed by a curtain of pines, Monsieur Montgrabel's superb aircottage was reposing softly, giving the impression of a huge basking shark.

A thread of smoke was rising into the blue. Already, the table had been laid for dinner in the open air, in the atmosphere of the littoral seaweeds and the coastal pines, between pretty blocks of ruddy rock, directly before the sun, which was declining with a slow majesty, extinguishing its radiance in the illuminated sea.

"Magnificent!" exclaimed Monsieur Montgrabel, leaping out of the miniplane. "I said so—it's beginning well."

"Splendid!" said Charles, with a child in each arm. "A well-chosen mooring. And a dinner that will be very welcome too!

"Why," said the amazed Monsieur Montgrabel, "is that you, Jean-Marie? You're no longer at Ouessant?"

A man costumed as a sailor emerged from a gap in the rocks and presented himself, cap in hand.

"Yes, Monsieur, it's me. I have a leave and I've come about the submersible..."

"Yes, yes, and to see Annette, no? That's very nice of you. You've seen the *Espadon* It's at Roscoff?"

"It's expecting you, Monsieur."

"That's perfect. Go and eat with the crew, and tomorrow morning, you can take us to the submarine."

XI. Beneath the Ocean with the submarine Espadon.
Agriculture and pisciculture

A delightful awakening in the cove of Kérouzéré.
Monsieur Montgrabel was up at six o'clock in the morning. He had spent a good night, dreaming that he had
finally realized an old plan that had haunted him for
many years—which is to say, the "ring canal," designed
to connect up all the navigable watercourses, thirty or
forty kilometers from the coasts or frontiers, ensuring
direct communication between all the regions, from
north to south and west to east, the Mediterranean basin,
the Loire basin, the Central Plateau, the plains of the
Nord, the plains of Alsace, etc...

In his dream, the impatient Montgrabel skipped
over all the labor, the ring canal advanced visibly. He
woke up amazed to find himself, not, as the thought, at

the solemn inauguration of an important stretch from the coast of Bordeaux to Arles, but on the shore of the Breton Sea, in a luxurious bedroom of his aircottage.

The later formed a beautiful bright mass on the little beach; the habitation, like a long nacelle, provided at the front and rear with balcony-verandas decked with climbing plants, was greatly extended by rooms to the left and right, by means of a system of extensible partitions, forming a port and starboard transept, with an additional upper trance in the central section. Breakfast was served on that terrace, before a considerably extended horizon. The entire family was soon gathered there. The children were eager to go and run over the sand and Annette, very agitated, was darting Sister Anne glances,[6] sometimes in the direction of Roscoff and sometimes toward Sibiril, impatient to see Jean-Marie emerging from a by-road.

As she was pouring white cream into the cups, an outburst of Monsieur Montgrabel's voice made her shudder. A little cream spilled on to the tablecloth because she turned round too abruptly, in order to direct a welcoming smile downwards.

"Well, Jean-Marie," said Monsieur Montgrabel, "have you alerted the *Espadon*?"

"Yes Monsieur; it's expecting you at the mooring in the harbor."

Jean-Marie arrived, swinging a large skate in his right hand and an enormous turbot in the left.

---

[6] The reference is to the Perrault version of "Barbe-Bleue" [Bluebeard], in which the curious wife stations her sister, Anne, as a lookout to warn her about her husband's return, and asks her repeatedly whether she can see anyone coming.

Monsieur Montgrabel and Charles were soon ready; they leapt on to the sand and, following in Jean-Marie's footsteps, headed overland toward the white bell-tower of Roscoff, shining amid the verdure in the distance.

In the little harbor, in front of Mary Stuart's house and the ruined chapel, Monsieur Montgrabel recognized the *Espadon*. It was a vessel of a very particular form, reminiscent of a large whale, carrying a bulbous tower on its back—a whale with two heads of course, one at the front and one at the back, and visible on each head, at the end of a muzzle elongated beneath the waves, were two enormous eyes, wide open, as if on the look-out. The turret also had two eyes looking at the coast. That made sox portholes—or, rather, six large round windows of reinforced crystal, which remained open upon the glaucous depths during dives, while the submarine wandered through the aquatic prairies.

With so many eyes, the *Espadon* had not failed to perceive the newcomers. Captain Guénard immediately appeared on deck, and sent a metal dinghy to fetch his passengers.

Captain Guénard was a man of about forty, tall and thin. A passionate ichthyologist, he took advantage of his submarine cruises in the waters of Brittany or the Norwegian fjords, the Mediterranean depths or the Archipelago, through the rocks of the Cyclades, to amass observations and interesting notes on the fauna or flora of the median depths unknown to travelers or excursionists on the surface.

"It's the first time you've visited the underside of the waves that come to beat our cliffs and rocks and unfurl on our beaches?" he said to the newcomers. "Then prepare yourselves for intense joys and all sorts of surprises...agreeable, Messieurs always agreeable, I hasten to assure you…and often amazing for the sagacious observer or the simple lover of picturesque distractions."

"Bravo!" said Monsieur Montgrabel. "I'm ready—we're ready!"

"The picturesque we shall have…perhaps too much for your taste—we'll see! Three of four years ago, I took one of my friends, an artist. He painted for eight hours a day; he made sketches outside, in a diving-suit, at a depth of twenty or twenty-five meters, or brushed studies inside, at the great portholes. He was sometimes all a-tremble with artistic emotion before the splendors of coloration and bushy entanglement of a submarine forest, through which fish strange in form and fabulous in color were galloping, if I might put it thus."

Monsieur Montgrabel had escaped gently in order inspect the accommodation of the *Espadon*. He had seen the cabins, sufficiently comfortable, although inevitably a trifle narrow. They would be more at ease in the lounge, in good armchairs, before the broad glass of the rear portholes, through which nothing could be seen for the moment but the background of the harbor, the Pointe de Primel with its brightly sunlit verdure, islets and white sails on the sea.

A lateral corridor to port led directly to the forward portholes. A watertight partition between the portholes could be closed instantaneously in case of necessity, thus securing the lounge from any accident. In the center of the submersible the lounge connected with the deck and the turret by means of a staircase that was rather steep but quite practicable, even for passengers.

Monsieur Montgrabel had soon concluded his inspection and declared himself satisfied. The ladies could come. One of the vessel's hydroplanes went to fetch them from the aircottage.

When they were aboard, the captain had lunch served. The ladies found that first day abroad the *Espadon* very agreeable and quite short. It is true that they were almost always navigating on the surface in calm weather, cruising within sight of the coast between Primel and Brigognan, except for an hour at sunset, a little further out at sea, in order to accustom the ladies to diving.

Afterwards, they slept well to the rhythmic lull of the waves—a restful night, even more tranquil than the one in the aircottage. Having consulted with Jean-Marie, Monsieur Montgrabel had settled his plans. In order to reach Jean-Marie's sector, where two or three submersibles were occupied in the work of clearance and adaptation, the *Espadon* set a course for Brest.

The vessel dived, with Jean-Marie Jézéquel aboard, now at home. They penetrated a region where extensive submarine prairies, previously ravaged by violent movements of the ea, had been cleared by dredging and sheltered for some time by protective constructions, huge sunken blocks forming points of support, connected by submarine breakwaters of reinforced concrete, and other works analogous to the constructions of defense against the devastating Alpine torrents.

Behind those defenses, the aquatic prairies were rapidly reconstituted. Already, the fish that had emigrated in search of new pastures were reappearing.

"Look, Monsieur! Do you see those algae out there, the bushes behind the breakwater? And further on, a little wood, a true forest where the fish are fluttering? Look, Mademoiselle Pierrette! A family of skates that are coming to look at us through the window! And over there, the conger eels in single file. Yes, Monsieur, we've begun to replant all that in only two years..."

All the marine plants had in fact, prospered. By pressing a button under the porthole, a beam of electric light illuminated the sea to a certain distance and permitting the perception of vast fields in which bouquets of large algae were swaying gently.

The submarine, which was moving slowly, went around those bushes, causing groups of fish to emerge from under rocks, amid splashes of sparks and foam. The silence around the vessel, in those aquatic plains where everything was stirring and swaying gently, was impressive. But Jean-Marie was loquacious, and the joyful children leapt abut, uttering exclamations, at ever change of scene.

Jean-Marie continued his picturesque explanations, which the captain occasionally completed with less summary technical details.

"In these submarine pastures, we nurture shoals of fish, much as flocks of sheep and herds of cattle are kept on the lands of Brittany or Cotentin: true salt-meadows, ours are, I can tell you!"

"Yes, as well as the results of methodical husbandry and good protection," the captain added, "we extract iodine, bromine and numerous other useful products from these maritime prairies..."

"And the nets that drag the sea regularly in the well-located regions, are no longer lowered by the old trawlerman who rakes blindly, and who ruins the sea-bed, no, it's necessary to see that, Monsieur, in the good places, the reservations...it's the miraculous catch every time! He doesn't suspect anything, the fish; he's tranquil, well-nourished and well-guarded—until the moment comes to go on to the land and into the frying-pan, naturally—sure that he'll no longer be swallowed by the porpoises. Oh, Monsieur, there are great porpoise-hunts nowadays, at sea off Douarnenez. You see here the husbandry and the protection; out there you'll not only see the protection, but us, the submarine shepherds..."

"We'll be there!" said Monsieur Montgrabel and Captain Guénard, simultaneously.

XII. A Porpoise Hunt on the Aquatic Prairies

In the ten days that they have been navigating at an average of twelve or fifteen meters beneath the waves, no one has experienced any boredom or disillusionment. Life aboard the *Espadon* goes by smoothly, in perfect indolence, before the portholes. The seabed views succeed one another with an unexpected variety, the aspect sometimes changing with an astonishing rapidity. Plains of low and bushy vegetation, only astonishing by virtue of its extraordinary coloration and the swarming of small species—sole, plaice, dabs or the warlike hosts of crabs—are succeeded by long sandbanks where sand-eels play, scintillating with silver flashes.

The submersible plays in the green waves and the white foam; it goes to explore deserted islets and previously-inaccessible grottoes. For some of those explorations, Monsieur Montgrabel and Charles put on the vessel's diving-suits and, guided by Jean-Marie, they take the risk of going outside the submersible, via the exit tube that opens alongside the engine-room, underneath the lounge.

The first time, it was a big surprise for the ladies and the children to see the strange figures of the excursionists appearing at the porthole. Gustave and Pierrette were frightened momentarily, but when they saw their father taking off the helmet and breathing-apparatus on returning, all fear disappeared, and when the second excursion took place Pierrette threw a violent temper tantrum because they refused to take her.

The *Espadon*, navigating on the surface in order to sniff the breeze and bathe in the sunshine, headed for a white column, sparkling on some rock lost in the mists of the horizon: a lighthouse indicating the route to surface vessels, a simple granite tower where two or three virtuous hermits of the sea resided, responsible for maintaining the protective beacon.

There, Monsieur Montgrabel suddenly remembered that he had a few urgent words to say, at a distance, to Paris, New York or Constantinople, and occupied the wireless post for hours, which the family employed in fishing parties around the islet.

They had already made one or two veritable ports of call. The aircottage had gone to wait for them at a point indicated by radio and sometimes, when they were navigating on the surface, it came to find the submarine, which took it in tow. How convenient that was! The aircottage either brought provisions from terra firma itself or sent them by hydroplane: butter and milk, vegetables and cutlets.

However, Suzanne was not tranquil; Charles's cold attitude remained disquieting. Ordinarily so expansive, during the excursions, he remained indifferent before the most admirable views, or even gave the impression of mulling over some tormenting thought that sometimes made him purse his lips dolorously.

One evening, a wireless telephone call announced the long-awaited porpoise hunt for the following day. The sardine- and tuna-fishers of Douarnenez had spotted numerous bands of those voracious cetaceans in the vicinity of Belle-Île, which were brazenly indulging in veritable massacres of nets and fish.

The *Espadon* resurfaced in order to travel quietly, by night, into the region of Belle-Île and take part in the operation at daybreak.

Two submersibles from Noirmoutiers were the first to reach the meeting-point; three others soon arrived from the station at Audierne. A conversation was engaged by radio. The fishermen from Audierne had had their nets badly damaged during the night by the frolicking porpoises, and the sardines, abundant in the previous days, had fled in disarray in an unknown direction.

Until nearly ten o'clock the watchmen surveyed the horizon in vain; no enemy was signaled.

Suddenly, a band of large animals, cetaceans of a good size, appeared directly ahead of the *Espadon*. They seemed to be springing forth from the foam, chasing one another without appearing to pay any heed to the submarine. They were capering and leaping, as if launched by springs, and then they dived into the dark green waves underneath the boat, to reappear some distance away on the other side.

"Fine beasts!" cried Jean-Marie. "Nearly two meters, the biggest, and the little ones, the young ones, leap as well as their parents. They're in the process of amusing themselves in order to build up an appetite…wait a moment, to see…here come the hunters, maneuvering!"

The submarines of the administration scattered, semi-submerged, steering in such a fashion as to reunite and encircle the troop. One submersible dived in order to drive upwards any prey that might have reached the depths, and gather it with the others.

The *Espadon* did the same, descending a few fathoms. The water was marvelously transparent; the searchlight illuminated, to a range of fifty meters, a vast sandy beach, extending in gently undulations. In the distance, as if in a liquid fog, the searchlight of the other submarine was perceptible, like a fugitive comet.

Suddenly, however, the transparency disappeared; the water darkened; then, after a few minutes, there was another change. One might have thought that the *Espadon* had suddenly entered a river of milk. Ahead, to either side, there was a silver stream, a white flow along the portholes, with a sort of murmur or splashing, perceptible to the ears.

"The sardines," said Jean-Marie.

It was, in fact, a large shoal of sardines, which the *Espadon* was cleaving with its hull: poor sardines, into the midst of which three dozen enormous porpoises plunged, jaws agape, sometimes disappearing in the mass, opening large breaches with thrusts of the tail.

Captain Guénard swerved sideways in order to leave the field free for the other submersible, which launched itself at the prey. A few muffled detonations were heard as the hunter opened fire. Porpoises bounded, turning upside down, agitating their fins spasmodically, and rising slowly toward the surface.

As the submarine reached the troop, seized by panic, everything almost disappeared in the midst of the turbulent water and the silvery flutter of sardines plastered against the portholes.

"Let's go back up," said the captain.

They resurface for the battle, and the *Espadon* found itself admirably placed in order not to miss anything of the tactics of the submarine shepherds or the episodes of the hunt. The troop of porpoises appeared at the surface, in a visible panic, spreading terror among those that had been frolicking unsuspectingly in the waves a moment before by means of their disorderly leaps.

The submarines, in a circle, advanced rapidly to place themselves within range.

"How are they armed?" asked Monsieur Montgrabel.

"With small cannon mounted like rocket-launchers, whose projectiles carry buoys designed to mark the places where wounded porpoises are struggling..."

"I hope we're going to play our part in the battle?"

"Certainly—look, the *Espadon* is armed."

Monsieur Montgrabel turned round. Two sailors were setting up on a long and slender cannon on the deck and preparing a crate of projectiles, all furnished with large cork floats at the end of a long cord.

"Fire!" said the captain.

Madame Montgrabel and Suzanne, who had also come up on deck, jumped. There was a flash and a puff of smoke immediately dispersed by the wind.

"*Touché!*" said the captain, Jean-Marie and Monsieur Montgrabel, simultaneously.

A porpoise coming straight toward the *Espadon* leapt into the air, to fall back flat on the waves, making the projectile's float dance.

"Reload quickly! Here come others, ready targets!"

The ladies, who had stayed on the last steps of the stairway, went down again rapidly in order to return to the portholes, half-bathed by the waves.

Rapidly aimed, the cannon fired again.

"*Touché* again!"

Aboard the other submarines too, not a minute was being wasted, nor a projectile.

Smoke rose up in rings into the sky, floats danced a saraband on the crests of the waves, among the porpoises in total disarray. Nothing could be distinguished but long tails and fins beating the foam, threads of water launched into the air by blow-holes, or the white bellies of the stricken, bobbing on the surface of the water, a darker green in the hollows of the waves.

Further away, agile arched silhouettes were fleeing, like the groups of dolphins in swirls of foam painted on ancient Greek vases, or the Japanese drawings of old Hokusai.

XIII. An Air-Land Village.

A magnificent day! Leaving a special boat of the shepherds of the sea to collect the dead animals, the submarines set off in pursuit of the survivors of the troop, which had escaped to the open sea.

Night was falling; a crescent moon was already shining when the *Espadon* and the aircottage discovered, in an inlet near Noirmoutier, a little to one side of the Bois de la Chaise, the ideal corner for repose after a day so well-employed. Next to a little stream descending to the sea through a wooded ravine, there was a veritable nest of verdure, completely sheltered from the sea breezes. They would sleep admirably there amid the soft rustle of foliage, mingled with the murmur of the waves.

"What calm! What silence! Oh, I count staying here for a few days," said Monsieur Montgrabel, when Captain Guénard had taken his leave to return to his vessel. "Tomorrow, I'll bask in the sun on the sand, like a lizard. No worries, no business affairs...oh, yes, one! I've thought about it already; it's necessary to get it under way immediately. Hey, Jean-Marie, come here for a moment!"

Jean-Marie did not take long to climb the stairway to the terrace. Monsieur Montgrabel took him to one side for five minutes. A few exclamations on the part of Jean-Marie were heard.

"Oh...! Ah...! Yes, Monsieur...! Of course, Monsieur! Oh, I'm very glad! Sure and certain...! And Annette, too!"

Monsieur Montgrabel returned to the family group.

"There," he said, "that's done. That's my last business deal...a little commerce in fish, turbots, crayfish, lobsters, etc. Not for me, for Jean-Marie. I'm going into partnership with him. First, I'll assure him of the establishment of his family; I'll send him all our friends. Now, I have a mind free of all preoccupation, I'm already asleep. I sense that it would require more cannon-shots fired in my ear to wake me up before eleven o'clock or noon tomorrow."

True to his word, Monsieur Montgrabel slept like a weary hunter until nine o'clock. It was not cannon-fire that woke him up but a little noise on the beach, the sound of voices and comings and goings on the veranda, and even the buzz of aircraft.

Still half-asleep, he drew his curtains and opened his window.

"What!" he said, rubbing his eyes. "Our inlet, deserted yesterday evening, our Crusoesque beach where I intended to sprawl in the sand in complete liberty, look at it now! But there's a crowd! But it's a town! Am I seeing things this morning, or have we flown away yesterday evening?"

Yes, the deserted inlet had become, if not a town, at least a little sea-side village, pretty and animated. Around the aircottage, four other elegant and over-elaborate airchalets, painted in bright colors with all their balconies florid, were lined up on the shingle, while a fifth was just settling on the rocks, almost on the water-line.

To his utter surprise, Monsieur Montgrabel recognized, in that fifth chalet, that of his son Maurice, the intensive agriculturalist, worldwide grocer, etc. Maurice was making signals to him from a facing window; a band of bare-legged children were running in front of the gentle waves that were unfurling all the way to the chalets. Pierrette and Gustave were already there, splashing one another enthusiastically.

But Monsieur Montgrabel was rapidly snatched from the pleasure of following their frolics, because the tele bell resounded. It was the clever sleuth that he had launched on the trail of the Boissy mystery, who was finally showing signs of life. Until now, the investigation had yielded no results. Had he discovered something this time?

Monsieur Montgrabel locked his door and, as a precaution, spoke into the apparatus in a low voice, muffling the loudspeaker.

"Well, what's new? A trail, some clue? That mysterious reporter…? Yes, that's right... Hello! What did you say? You suspect Monsieur Blossière, who was one of my twenty-four secretaries for a time? I had to deprive myself of his services. Oh, he's dabbling in feminist politics now? I remember…a lady-killer devoured by ambition... Hello! If I knew his forename? Eh? His name is Camille! Oho! Camille Blossière, Camille Boissy... Ah! He's just written a eulogistic article on the book in question, you say? Five or six electoral subscriptions already want to send this Camille Boissy to the Chamber… Let's see, do you have Monsieur Blossière's address? Ah! Montrouge, the quarter of the letter…Office 48, Montrouge! Until tomorrow—I need to reflect...?"

Reflect was easy enough to say. At eleven o'clock, twenty-four parasols could be counted, planted at the limit of the waves, and fifty deckchairs occupied by women. Hydroplanes arrived from Pornic were hovering above the waves, accompanying the *Espadon*, which were bringing friends for a little diving tour around Noirmoutier.

Visits succeeded one another at the aircottage. Monsieur Montgrabel went back and forth between the veranda where Madame Montgrabel and Suzanne were receiving, and the drawing room, where Maurice and Charles, with Monsieur Larose, weighted down by an enormous portfolio, had taken their places around a heap of circulars, letters and various papers.

Monsieur Montgrabel distributed handshakes and amiable but brief remarks to the visitors, and then went back to dive into the heap of messages, which he scanned and then passed to one or other of his sons.

"Up to you…up to you…," he said. "It's your affair now…"

There were further visits, polite remarks and handshakes. Monsieur Montgrabel came back again...

"Hang on, what's this? *Electoral committee, mixed intellectual section, Var et Bouches-du-Rhône!* Madame Charles Montgrabel! It's for Suzanne..."

"Var et Bouches-du-Rhône?" said Monsieur Larose. "In that regard, I have various things to communicate to you..."

"Again, Madame Charles Montgrabel... Madame Charles... Another Committee... Madame... Another..."

"Give them to me!" said Charles, in a changed voice, while Suzanne disappeared.

"But who's that fellow over there coming toward us?" said Monsieur Montgrabel, suddenly. "I know him...it's..."

Monsieur Larose had turned round. "It's my secretary," he said. "A talented fellow, Monsieur Blossière, an advocate and journalist..."

"Blossière? Camille Blossière, one of my own former secretaries..."

"Oh, he's been in your employ? He's now in mine," said Larose, laughing. "Does it annoy you that I've brought him?"

"Not at all—on the contrary... Wait a minute, I'll come back."

At the mere mention of Blossière's name, Charles had shuddered and had stood up abruptly, frowning, his face distressed. Monsieur Montgrabel grabbed his arm and drew him into another room, not without having glanced into the drawing room. Suzanne had not flinched; doubtless she had not perceived Blossière.

Monsieur Blossière, whom Montgrabel had described as a "lady-killer" a few minutes earlier, was a fellow of thirty or thirty-five, handsome and rather elegant in appearance, with an expression of expansive satisfaction in which he was smiling into his neatly-groomed blonde beard.

"So, Charles," said Monsieur Montgrabel, "I see you're up to date..."

"I arrived at the tele the other day when you were talking with Paris about that accursed Poste Restante envelope. I didn't say anything, although I could have. Immediately, though, I thought about Blossière. Why? I don't know...or rather, I recalled that he had had a rapport with Suzanne on social occasions at the house. Is it him, the correspondent...the man of the letters? What audacity! Coming to confront us here! But I'm exaggerating...there certainly can't have been any imprudence on the part of Suzanne. I wanted to demand a frank explanation from her, but I recoiled before the odiousness of the suspicions. And yet, if I can't hold myself back, I'll go seize that man by the collar and throw him out!"

"Calm down," said Monsieur Montgrabel. "We'll soon know. Wait!"

He opened the door to the drawing room.

"Monsieur Larose, a word, if you please. I have something to ask you."

Monsieur Larose, in discussion with his secretary regarding the papers the latter had brought, hastened to arrive, papers in hand.

"You say, Monsieur Montgrabel, that you have something to ask me?"

"Yes, a very small thing. Could you show me a specimen of your secretary's handwriting?"

"*Our* secretary," said Larose, laughing. "So you practice graphology—that's good. Here, these notes are his—a few proposed declarations on various subjects..."

Monsieur Montgrabel cast a rapid glance over the papers. He had a surprised expression; then, after riffling through them, he returned them to Monsieur Larose, only keeping the last sheet.

"Excuse me—I'll be back in a minute..."

He went to his room, immediately followed by Charles, who left Monsieur Larose impolitely to his own devices, without even thinking of excusing himself.

"I have the envelope, we'll soon see. But I'm surprised, it seems to me that this handwriting bears no resemblance to...let's see...where are my papers? Wait..."

In order to assist his father, Charles searched feverishly though a few files that Monsieur Montgrabel had just taken out of a drawer.

"Wait, wait, you'll muddle everything up...ah, here it is? Well, no, a simple glance suffices. Complete error...entirely different handwriting. Blossière isn't the correspondent!"

XIV. The Great Affair of the Puy-de-Dôme
The Inauguration Banquet
of the Synthetic Factories

There was one major enterprise of the company, or, rather, two: firstly, the works for the utilization of the Puy de Dôme; secondly, the great affair of Monsieur Valette's synthetic factories: a fine idea, which presented enormous difficulties of execution.

The Puy de Dôme was being pierced in order to pour into it a diversion of the Allier and extract torrents of steam therefrom, which gigantic turbines would utilize to the great benefit of the region, transformed into a great industrial center.

There had been strong opposition to the idea, with, it has to be admitted, rather powerful arguments: *Scien-*

tific imprudence! Dangerous folly! Will inevitably bring about disasters of catastrophes, and the ruination of all the surrounding terrain, etc. In spite of all those objections and in the teeth of all the hostility, Monsieur Montgrabel had persisted. There had not been any catastrophe, or even a serious accident; and the success of the "dangerous folly" now seemed complete.

The Puy de Dôme—"the old volcano that had been allowed to die out," as a individual named Labiche[7] had called it, in the last century—had, therefore, been pierced. That was the easy part of the enterprise, successfully executed.

At the same time, the work of diversion, carefully planned, had made rapid progress. A tube-canal took a portion of the waters of the Allier, collected those of a few small steams encountered in the way, solely to the detriment of a few families of frogs, and brought them to the Puy de Dôme.

Artful construction works on a considerable scale had been carried out: hydraulic factories, pumping stations, redistribution plants... Everything had gone well, in spite of the anticipated difficulties, and even the unanticipated ones, and on a fine day, in the previous spring, the regional prefect of Auvergne and the Central Plateau, by pressing a button in the director's office of the last pumping station established on the side of the mountain at an altitude of even hundred meters—a magnificent construction of metal and reinforced concrete in a remarkably picturesque ensemble—had projected into the flank of the swollen old volcano, more amazed than in-

---

[7] The playwright Eugène Labiche (1815-1868), in *Le Misanthope et l'Auvergnat* (1852).

convenienced, the thousands of cubic meters of water brought by the tube-canal.

At a distance, they waited, quivering with anxiety. There was a formidable noise, rumbling and groaning, the amplitude of which seemed to grow and multiply, and then came the decrescendo of plunge into the entrails of the Earth. But there was no explosion, no eruption, no catastrophe, and not the smallest accident. The lid of the Puy de Dôme was not blown off. Clermont-Ferrand respired. The insurance companies, which had indemnified the town for that circumstance, did not have to regret their confidence.

Through the orifices prepared in a crown around the old volcano, the steam started to rise toward the heavens in large white swirls, which eventually came together and mingled.

Those inexhaustible torrents of steam were not to be lost in the clouds of the sky; they were to power Monsieur Valette's synthetic factories, and all those that were to surge forth in the surrounding area.

The success of that great enterprise was proclaimed in all the scientific journals and is being celebrated today at the great banquet of the inauguration of the "steam-powered derivative of the perforated Puy de Dôme." The entire Montgrabel family is there, having disembarked from the dirigible the previous evening.

"I shall not say any more, Messieurs, about the endeavor that has won the admiration of all the prominent people gathered around this table, celebrities of science, high finance, art and industry, a social elite who ornament this manifestation of a splendid banquet with grace and elegance..." (*Bravo! Bravo!*) "...And I raise my glass to the splendid success of this enterprise of genius. I drink to its promoters, to all the laborers and men of science to whom we owe this magnificent endeavor, to the man who carried it through, to all the agents of progress!"

That is the prefect of the Auvergne finishing his speech. An audience of the highest quality, the prefect has said, eminent people of every order, guests from all sectors of society, the political world, the academies, great industry, representatives of the press... A superb banquet, highly successful, to which a group of well-known gourmets has been invited and placed at an immense table of honor, writers of "*haulte graisse*," practicing Rabelaisians and stars of the hospitality industry. And everyone at that table of honor seems to be overflowing with delirious enthusiasm, making a great deal of noise. Motions are proposed, toasts drunk; everyone raises his glass joyfully, and the prefect has requested.

"...Marvelous, your factories! Superbly equipped!"

"The Puy de Dôme is seething and fuming! Long live the old Puy and those who have reignited it...!"

"...For the greater good of the surrounding region and..."

"A marvelous tableau, that ensemble of the Puy du Dôme, with the adduction tubes, those fabulous platform and all that extraordinary apparatus...and the plumes of smoke..."

"Excellent, the cuisine! First class menu..."

"Succulent! All supremely exquisite: ducklings, roast pheasants, salmon trout, etc... Everything, absolutely everything..."

"And the wines! Superior, all the wines! All of them, a delightful bouquet, a frankness..."

"But how was it done? Not a single bone in the chicken, in the pheasant...all so carefully filleted..."

"Not a single pip in the apples, the pears, the grapes..."

"Long live Valette!"

"Valette! Valette! Valette!"

"Monsieur Valette has the floor," pronounced the president.

A salvo of applause welcomed Monsieur Montgrabel's son-in-law when, obedient to the appeal, he rose to his feet...

"An ovation! An ovation!"

Three ovations burst forth, in which the table of honor took part, without sparing the hands. They acclaimed Valette, Madame Valette, Monsieur Montgrabel, science, industry, etc..."

Monsieur Valette declared that he was not an orator, and assured the audience, showing them a piece of paper, that they need not dread a long speech. He would only summarize, in a few sentences, the great work, the endeavor, his goal, his methods, his immediate results and his anticipations...

We shall pass over the details, in spite of their interest, in order to arrive more rapidly at the final explanations.

"Finally, Mesdames et Messieurs, I'll conclude... How did you find our banquet? Your applause leads me to think that you are not too discontented. I can see, not far away from me, the expansive faces of fine gastronomes, eminent specialists in the art of fine living, who appeared to me to be manifesting a certain enthusiasm just now..." (*Yes! Yes! Bravo!*) "They were truly exquisite, I dare say, the dishes we have just savored, were they not? That's your honest opinion...? Your satisfaction fills me with joy. Well, the salmon trout, the ducklings *à la française*, the roast lamb, the ruffled chicken, the pheasant *au chaud-froid*, etc…all those delicate dishes so warmly appreciated were purely and simply products of our synthetic factories, uniquely synthetic." (*Profound sensation.*)

"No veritable pheasant, no true pre-salted fillet, no trout, no duckling and no authentic chicken entered into the saucepans of the illustrious restaurateur who has magisterially realized our abundant menu. The entire menu was artificial and synthetic. Chemistry has furnished us with everything by synthesis, including the cheeses, in which you have encountered the particular taste and perfumes of the most celebrated natural cheeses of the region, and even the superb fruits of the dessert…"

The guests looked at one another; the bravos, momentarily constrained by the surprise of that revelation, resumed, in isolation at first, but then bursting forth again all along the tables.

"Yes, Messieurs, by synthesis! The wines themselves! I took note of the admiring comments just now: *Perfect, this Saint-Emilion! Remarkable, this Beaune! This champagne is more than sympathetic!* Well, the Saint-Emilion, the Pouilly, the Beaune and the champagne are all *synthesis 1965.* There, Messieurs! It is, therefore, the absolute triumph of chemistry, the absolute triumph of synthesis!" (*Explosion of bravos.*) "The suspicions, prejudices and preconceptions with which our synthetic factories collided, all fall in confrontation with the results. I hasten to say that the ridiculous pretention, emitted by certain people, to administer nourishment in chemical pills legitimates those suspicions perfectly…"

"Down with the pills!" proffered indignant voices in all the groups."

"Our synthetic factories do not manufacture pills, they furnish veritable foodstuffs, the synthesis of vegetable or animal products with all their particular elements and characteristics: flesh, fruits, vegetables, exactly as nature has the old habit of constituting them. But our synthetic products add to the solid basis of natural elements demanded of virtuous nature and transformed by chemistry, elements that we are going to extract from the great primal reservoir of strength and vital energy: the sea, which furnished the universal protoplasm, in the early ages of the globe." (*Long murmur of enthusiasm and a salvo of bravos.*)

It's definitely the algae, thought Monsieur Montgrabel. *Valette's secret agents went in search of them in Jean-Marie's world.*

"The vegetation of the immense prairies that carpet the bed of the oceans, the scorned and thus-far disdained fields, the great family of wrack and fucus, in innumerable varieties, the algae, simultaneously flesh and vegetable, furnish us with that solid basis..."

Monsieur Valette concluded his speech. The acclamations prevented his explanations from reaching the extremities of the hall. A complete success for the synthetic factories, the battle won. As the coffee was served, Monsieur Montgrabel called out to the "synthetic son-in-law": "My dear Valette, the coffee is synthetic too, I assume?"

"The coffee and the liqueurs, they're all synthetic," replied Valette.

"Very good! Long live synthesis!"

"One final word, Messieurs! For a very long time, science has been seriously preoccupied with the exceedingly grave question of nourishment. The development of the population of the poor Earth rendered the problem more anguishing every day: how could we exact, from a soil fatigued in places, the quantities of primary materials demanded by the appetite of the excessively numerous masses? Well, thanks to the synthetic factories, which we are going to see created and multiplied everywhere, those somber preoccupations are vanishing..."

XV. A Field of Social Experimentation.

"What a delightful son-in-law that dear Valette is!" said Monsieur Montgrabel, lighting an excellent synthetic cigar. "Yes, certainly, he truly is the synthesis of all the perfections desirable in a son-in-law! Speeches, toasts, factory visits, explanations on the spot, he takes all the difficulties upon himself, and I no longer have anything to do but relax. I've ordered the autos for two o'clock, after lunch. Oh, if all our affairs went as well as this one, what tranquility we'd have! But there'll still be hindrance, I sense it. Anyway, in the meantime, let's relax! Come on, Charles, have a cigar; let's set the black ideas aside. There'll be time to resume worrying in Paris. Monsieur Larose will leave, taking away that poor Monsieur Blossière, whose face remains disagreeable to us in spite of everything. Let's relax!"

Charles was about to ply when an employee came in and deposited an enormous stack of papers on the directorial desk.

"What's all this?" demanded Monsieur Montgrabel.

"Your correspondence, Monsieur—letters, wireless messages, newspaper cuttings, etc."

"Damn! Still persecuted here!

Monsieur Montgrabel made a start on the mass of persecuting messages. As he scanned the letters and messages or listened on the little apparatus on the desk to the phonograph disks, a crease furrowed his brow, and the back lock of hair above it twisted into several curls.

Twenty-five letters screwed up into balls went into the waste paper baskets under the desk or to the side; twenty-five messages were put to one side, abruptly annotated in pencil, as if by sword-thrusts. Montgrabel bounded to the tele two or three times for rapid communications and then resumed opening envelopes; then he rang again to summon one of his divisional chiefs.

"Well, what can you tell me about the Consumer Societies?"

"The movement is growing, Monsieur; leagues are forming to struggle against the trusts and the cartels..."

"That's all right, the market will equilibrate..."

"It would appear...it's said...that they're ideas highly recommended in a recent book, *The House...*"

"*...hold of the Nation.* I know."

"Now, a syndicate of those leagues has formed, which has voted as honorary president, the author, Monsieur Boissy, and with every passing minute, proposals are arriving here from Committees, telegrams and demands, for Monsieur Boissy..."

"Not known!"

"That's what I'm tired of repeating—but the syndicate persists; it advises me that tomorrow, a delegation will come to beg Monsieur Camille Boissy to accept that honorable presidency."

"Send that delegation away, energetically!"

"An exclamation from Charles interrupted him. Monsieur Montgrabel turned round. Charles had risen to his feet, very pale, dropping a heap of files and Monsieur Montgrabel's briefcase. The latter cut off the communication swiftly.

"Well, what? What is it now?"

"The letters!" said Charles.

"The letters? What letters?"

"The Poste Restante letters! Here they are...in the synthetic factories file."

"The file...that I brought from Paris. That's true. The same envelopes. I knew that there was something else in that famous handbag! Where was my head? I remember perfectly. When the object was brought to me, I as settling a few details with Valette with regard to these factories, and I must have inadvertently stuck those in the file. Too many affairs! What a tumultuous life, my poor Charles! CeBy, Office 48. That's the one. Let's see..."

No, Father, leave it—it's me who ought to..."

Charles leaned on the desk, not daring to look at the letters that he was holding in a tremulous hand. Finally, he made a decision, went to the window and slowly drew out a piece of paper from the first envelope.

"Well?" said Monsieur Montgrabel.

Charles shook the envelopes. A dozen letters fell out, which he picked up without saying a word, throwing them to his father after having scanned the first lines.

In his turn, Monsieur Montgrabel no longer dared look at them.

"You're very pale! You're trembling! So...these letters...?

"Innocent, Father, everything there is of the most innocent. Covering letters for proofs of the book, letters from the publisher, notification of going to press. At the last moment, Suzanne hesitated to allow it to appear. What emotion! What folly, too, on our part! My poor Suzette!"

Charles was red-faced now, and wiped his forehead.

"Poor, dear Suzette! To suppose her capable of...oh, I was mad and I don't know how I can ever be forgiven!"

"Fundamentally," said Monsieur Montgrabel, "I was quite certain that it would all be cleared up...but we're being summoned to lunch. I feel an appetite..."

"What about me, then?" cried Charles. "No, I'm no longer hungry."

The lunch, also synthetic, was quickly expedited, for the auto-flyers could be heard purring in the court-yard. Suzanne had an agreeable surprise. Charles, so morose in the morning, exhibited an extraordinary cheerfulness; he talked a great deal, ecstatic about the superb appearance of the children, the excellence of the synthetic boiled eggs and the blue of the sky...

Suzanne gazed at him in astonishment, amazed by the sudden but fortunate change of mood.

"By the way, where are we going?" asked Madame Montgrabel.

"Fifty or sixty kilometers," Charles replied, "to the arrondissement of La Bastide...a trip arranged yesterday..."

"Nice landscapes? Something good?"

"How should I know? Probably something picturesque and diverse."

"You know very well, my dear Madame," said Monsieur Larose. "The Statist experiment we were talking about? It's there. Have you forgotten?"

"We've all forgotten," said Charles. "It's the prefect who reminded us about it yesterday. I owe him gratitude, it will occupy the end of our vacation nicely...for our vacation is coming to an end..."

"Alas!" sighed Madame Montgrabel.

"I'm in haste to get back," said Suzanne, returning to her idea of writing a refutation of her book in order to deny everything, and already turning over in her mind ingenious means of saying exactly the opposite of what the odious Boissy had written. I need to get back...a little task..."

"No, no! We're not in any hurry!" exclaimed Charles. "Let's go to La Bastide!"

"Yes," said Monsieur Larose, "that arrondissement between the Lot and the Garonne, perhaps a little closer to the Garonne, is an ardent and active region, won over the Statist ideas a long time ago. In order to demonstrate the value of their theories, the doctrinaires of the party

loudly demanded an experimental field. The arrondissement of La Bastide solicited the honor of becoming that
field of experimentation. Very shrewd, the Bastidois!
You'll see!"

"We'll see!"

"As for me, I'm returning to Paris, I have to
work…and in the meantime, you know, I'm occupied
with the bearded philosopher…the famous author of the
Household. I believe I've got him, this time."

"Very good," said Monsieur Montgrabel. "Carte
blanche!"

"And good luck!" exclaimed Charles, laughing,
while Suzanne, to hide her disturbance, went to put her
children into the big autoflyer.

Everyone took their places. There was Monsieur
and Madame Montgrabel, Laurence Clifton, Marcelle
Valette, Charles, Suzanne and the two children.
Charles's usual pilot took the wheel of the large, solid
and sturdy autoflyer. The route was god, with only a few
towns and villages and a few steep hills to fly over in
order to cut he journey to a minimum.

Charles simultaneously joyful and desolate, won-
dered in vain how he was going to enable the bad days,
whose cause he dared not admit, to be forgotten. He
kissed the children, and burst forth with a flood of words
that amazed Suzanne.

The auto-flyer sped along the road, but at every
moment some location that merited being seen at closer
range appeared to the right or the left soliciting the gaze.
What was a little detour for an autoflyer? A matter of a
simple leap. And the autoflyer rose up, quit the road,
bounding over a clump of trees, crossed a river or the
ridge of a hill forty meters in the sir, in order to land
again at the glimpsed site, sometimes a rocky gorge

winding into a mountainous massif, a fine winding ravine, the ruin of a château with broken towers surging forth above wild bushy slopes, or a small town of feudal appearance with old building packed into a corset of almost-intact ramparts, with no flightpad amid its steeples and turrets, only a modest tube-station to mark the century.

After so many detours and stops, it was only in the evening that they reached La Bastide, an old industrial town, more contemporary in appearance that anything they had encountered on the way.

The little surprises of the route had caused Statism to be forgotten, and the scarcely gave it a thought when they arrived at the Lion d'Argent, the foremost hotel in the town. The dinner bell rang and the open air had given everyone an appetite.

There were not many people at the host's table—a few travelers arrived by tube. After having done honor to the first courses, the Montgrabel family felt better.

XVI. The Triumph of Monsieur Larose

Four days have already been spent in La Bastide. The region is charming; one would forget the Statist experiment if placards of all colors did not provide reminders of it everywhere, announcing meetings of various Social Study Circles, lectures, etc.

Monsieur Montgrabel is no longer thinking of requesting clarifications, for unfortunately, correspondence, the tele and wireless messages arrive continually to demand his presence at the Lion d'Argent.

The annoyances persist. He does not breathe a word about them, but they can be divined by the lock of black hair that twists above his forehead. Suzanne also receives messages, to which she does not respond. Charles remains light-hearted. He has, in any case, enough to do to maintain calm and cheerfulness, with the aid of the children and Marcelle Valette.

The autoflyer runs over the roads: agreeable explorations, but in the smallest villages, on the walls or even on the trees, one cannot help perceiving the Statists' placards and posters.

"Good! The paternal State can adopt us too. Five or six children more or less is nothing," said Charles, returning from the last excursion before the departure. Tell me, Father, have you retained the explanations? Don't the tourists passing through have to be nourished like the Bastidois?"

"My brain's too fuliginous to recall," replied Monsieur Montgrabel. "We'll see. Tomorrow morning, to clarify the point, I'll refuse to pay the hotel bill."

That final evening, there is no correspondence at all. A breakdown of all services. Charles rubs his hands. Suzanne breathes more easily. But Monsieur Montgrabel, who complains about being harassed by messages, seems discontented not to have any.

Monsieur Montgrabel has just given the pilot of the autoflyer the program for the departure: join the main line tube at Périgueux and return to Paris by the express; telephone this evening to reserve a special compartment.

"What!" protested Madame Montgrabel. "We're not going back to the aircottage, which we sent to Royan to wait for us? Our vacation is going to be limited, then, to a few paltry weeks spent with the worthy Jean-Marie's submarine shepherds, the inauguration of the factories, and banquets?"

"We'll see, my dear. We can put the aircottage on the lawn in front of the house in Paris, and you can move into it to finish the season..."

In the morning, no post again, nor any other communication. Monsieur Montgrabel has something akin to hunger pangs in his head. He paces back and forth in his room while Annette and the pilot take care of the luggage.

Suddenly, at eleven o'clock, the breakdown of the tele comes to an end, and the wireless messages arrive. They learn the reason for the breakdown. Yesterday evening a meeting of the employees of the local Administrations of the Post, the Tele, the Radio, etc., demanding a six-hour day, decreed that the offices would open for a week, by way of a trial, from eleven a.m. to five p.m., which does indeed add up to six hours—including the lunch hour, of course.

When Monsieur Montgrabel saw the avalanche of messages, and heard the tele bells and the voices of employees distributing numbers to the communications. He told the pilot to leave the autoflyer and the luggage, the departure having been postponed.

Oh, yes, the breakdown was over and the flood flowed in: the previous day's and today's. Monsieur Montgrabel set aside for Charles everything that appeared to be business correspondence; that was no longer his concern. He listened to and cut short a number of communications. An appeal from the tele, repeated several times, caused him to hasten the clearance.

It was Monsieur Larose who was ringing. He appeared in the screen of the tele, his expression visibly satisfied, cordiality in his lips.

"Finally, my dear Monsieur, I've encountered you. I've been ringing since yesterday evening. How are you? Yes, yes, I know, it was blocked. Oh, these Statist employees! The ladies are well? Are they content with the little excursion? Interesting, isn't it? Well, I too am content, delighted...everything is arranged."

"What?"

"The Camille Boissy affair. I'm glad to be able to announce to Madame Charles Montgrabel that she can sleep tranquilly henceforth. No one will annoy her any longer with that Boissy. The journalistic investigation was very badly conducted. They have however, a good track. The bald and bearded philosopher is..."

"His name is unimportant," said Monsieur Montgrabel, uttering a sigh of relief. Wait a minute while I call my daughter-in-law to the apparatus, to tranquilize her too, poor child..."

In a corner of the lounge to one side, Suzanne, with Pierrette on her knees, was transcribing a few notes. In response to her father-in-law's summons, she ran to the tele.

"Bonjour, Madame! Happy to present you with my compliments," said Monsieur Larose.

"My dear Suzanne, you've had many annoyances caused by a certain Monsieur Boi...Monsieur Larose has succeeded in discovering the author of the wretched book. The search has been vain, until now. This Boissy really is a bald and bearded old gentleman..."

"Old but not as old as all, that," protested Monsieur Larose, "merely mature, slightly balding, yes, and somewhat bearded, in fact, to replace a few missing hairs..."

"So, my little Suzette, don't worry. No one will torment you any longer, henceforth. The newspapers have spoken, and they've even published the portrait of the real Camille Boissy. Ah, it's noon! *Le Flambeau* ought to have arrived in La Bastide. Would you be kind enough to go and fetch it?"

"I've just seen it on the table in the lounge," said Suzanne, eagerly. "I'll bring it right away, Father."

"I'm very grateful to you, Monsieur Larose, for having brought the affair to a successful conclusion..."

"I've done it for the best. In any case, I've already been occupied with it for some time, seeking the best solution. I've thought about it a great deal. I've seen many people..."

Suzanne came back in with the newspaper unfolded, her facing registering a certain surprise.

"Let's see this Boissy!" said Monsieur Montgrabel, extending his hand. "Let's see this modest an mysterious philosopher, fearful of bright light and renown."

Suzanne seemed to hesitate. Monsieur Montgrabel had to get up in order to take the newspaper.

"Well?" he said. "What's so curious, then, in *Le Flambeau*? Good, a long article on the front page, a sensational interview: *The real C. B.* Good. And the portrait... What? What? The real Boissy...but this is you, Monsieur Larose. It's you!"

"I have unveiled myself," said Monsieur Larose, smiling. "It is indeed me. Circumstances have led me to emerge from the discretion that I imposed upon myself initially. Now, I've confessed... You must read the article, full of interest. There are already notes in several other papers. The entire press will report..."

Monsieur Montgrabel appeared as surprised as Suzanne, and scanned the sensational interview.

"You've guessed correctly," Monsieur Larose continued. "Philosopher, I claim that title: I've acquired it in the observation of men and things, a little practical philosophy..."

"Certainly!" said Monsieur Montgrabel. "All my compliments, my dear Monsieur Larose. I see that it's a settled matter. But have you thought that the theories of Camille Boissy might hamper you a little, in your role as secretarial spokesman?"

"I didn't think of that at first; when I realized it, it was too late to search for another Boissy; I must continue to sacrifice myself. So. I'm obliged to ask you to accept my resignation. Believe that I'm infinitely sorry!"

"I'm as sorry as you are...but tell me, then, according to *Le Flambeau*, you're standing in the imminent elections...?"

"People have come to seek me in my retirement," said Monsieur Larose, modestly. "Yes, from several directions I've been solicited, pursued and tracked to drag me into Parliament. You are looking at a man literally quartered. On the one hand, the Feminist Party in Paris and in the Midi is covering me with flowers; on the other, various advanced intellectual sections..."

"Well, my dear Monsieur Larose, all my compliments...and all my thanks! Yes, no more committees, nor sub-committees, no program to discuss...a true relief! It's curious how I seem, suddenly, to be breathing more freely!"

Suzanne, very emotional had run away some time ago, and Charles came to the tele in his turn as the communication reached its end.

"Yes, the affair is concluded," Monsieur Montgrabel replied to Charles's questions. "Monsieur Larose has taken charge of it. He's a man full of wisdom. He's regulated everything in the best fashion...oof...! By the way, Charles, I've reflected a great deal during these long, very long days of repose, slightly stagnant in my opinion. And I've been thinking about what I said to you the other day—you know about my search for a small, tranquil occupation, well within my compass, in order to occupy my leisure? You remember? Well, I've discovered that I was mistaken, and...yes, I've changed my mind. Monsieur Larose has rendered me a true service. I'm going back into business. That's it, my tranquil little occupation, well within my compass!"

"Of course! I knew it," said Charles, laughing, while Madame Montgrabel looked up anxiously at her husband. "We're waiting for you, Father!"

"I've ceded the business to you, I won't go back on that. Except that, as I need to do something, would you like me as deputy director? Look, I sense that I'm already quite alert at the idea; my fortified intellect is vibrating more forcefully, I'm reviving! How many thanks I owe Monsieur Larose! Long live Larose! He's a great man... yes, I feel alive again...

"Come on, is it agreed. Am I deputy director?"

"You are."

"Good. A few little ideas occurred to me the other day, which I shall submit to the first board meeting. And I'll go back to Paris immediately to take up my position..."

"That settles everything," said Charles. "Since the deputy director of the company will be in his office in Paris tomorrow, the director can extend his vacation by a few days, for I too have an idea for the return... I've exposed it to Mother and Marcelle, who will be kind enough to take charge of bringing the children back to the house. You don't see any inconvenience in that little plan, Father?"

"None. Anyway, you need a breather after your voyages to Java and other places with excessive climates."

"And then too, Suzanne has been a little tormented lately."

"Mistakenly!" said Monsieur Montgrabel. "Poor little Suzanne, so lovely and sweet."

"Mistakenly, for sure," Charles went on, "but it's over now. So, in order to put it behind us completely, instead of coming back by tube with you like people in a hurry, Suzanne and I will take the schoolboy route. We'll escape, flee, all alone" In order to come back we're going to go donkeying..."

"What's that?"

"It's a new sport. Our generation is very sporty, you know. There are people wary of various overly practical and overly organized forms of tourism, overly familiar ports, autos, airplanes, aerial, submarine or mixed dirigibles; it's seekers of the unknown, avid for new impressions, who have invented donkeying. They've rediscovered the donkey, the worthy little donkey, the humble ass, a forgotten animal, almost lost. Oh, there's something to be done with the donkey! It's quite simple, you'll understand: one puts a saddle on it, with a bridle and stirrups, as people once did with horses. One climbs on to it, quite at ease, and one sets off, straight ahead, not on the cluttered, unapproachable, redoubtable roads, much too well-known, but tranquil little paths, gently and peacefully, over hills and vales, through fields and meadows, over grass or through brushwood, where the mount chews thistles in passing, along rivers with flowery banks, under poplars or in the coolness of shady woods. What do you think of our plan? It will be delightful along the banks of the Dordogne."

"Delightful. But where will you find the donkeys?

"I've had difficulty, but I've found three."

"Why three?"

"Two for us and one for the luggage. We'll go with you to the tube station in a little while, then Firmin will leave the auto-flyer in the garage and take the third donkey. I think he's perfectly capable of piloting a donkey,

150

even a recalcitrant one, such as one sometimes encounters, according to ancestral memories..."

"Go on, then, go donkeying, my children. Now let's have lunch, and afterwards, the tube to Paris. It's astonishing how alert and well I feel now, with an appetite for work!"

"Yes," said Madame Montgrabel, still anxious. "But I'm handing in my resignation..."

"That's understood. You'll only keep the departments of social relations. Look—another advantage of the new plan. Charles, as managing director, is constrained to leave major study voyages to others. He stays in Paris, no longer budging from his directorial office. Suzanne, delighted, isn't bored any more. Everything has worked out for the best!"

A smile illuminated Suzanne's face, serene again, and she kissed her father-in-law as a sign of reconciliation and gratitude.

"I think so!" said Monsieur Montgrabel, cheerfully. "It seems to me that I read yesterday on a poster, that according to the calculations of Statist statisticians, the State the great administrator, could, by means of a contribution of one franc ninety-eight per person per day, ensure all services, including those of nourishment and administration. We'll propose that figure to the hotelier of the Lion d'Argent!"

"And then to Paris," said Charles, "you by tube, us by the schoolboy route."

L'Ile des Centaures

des

Texte & Dessins

de

A Robida

Paris. — Henri LAURENS, Éditeur

6, Rue de Tournon, 6

CENTAUR ISLAND

I. Captain Zephyrin's Shipwreck and
Truly Extraordinary Encounter on an Unknown Shore

Long-haul captain Zephyrin Canigousse, of the port of Bordeaux, is not one of those mariners who allow themselves to be carried away by their imagination in recounting their travels and willingly embroider the truth. There was certainly never a man more worthy of faith. That love of decoration is good for the men of Marseille, but the captain is a native of Gascony, so one can believe him when he deigns to narrate some episode of his distant peregrinations.

Now, this is what Zephyrin Canigousse consented to tell us the other day, while picking fruits in the garden of his little house at Hendaye.

Not a single word will be changed in his story, told in a tone so simple, with a sight Gascon accent, mingled with that of the most perfect sincerity. We shall not add a single comma in scrupulously transcribing his words and we can affirm in advance that the worthy captain's truly amazing revelations will provoke a considerable emotion throughout the world and confound all scholars.

So (the captain began) we had left Melbourne and we were heading toward ****—the place name is irrelevant—when, after several weeks of tranquil navigation in increasingly warm and unfrequented regions, where we did not encounter anyone, even Malay pirates or savage pirogues, the weather suddenly got worse.

The sun continued to grill us, and it was a rotisserie and a boiler, along with the sea, that poured cataracts of hot water over our poor vessel. Suddenly, there was a cyclone, a frightful typhoon. Our ship was carried away like a wisp of straw, precipitated into the hollows of monstrous waves, thrown keel in the air into whirlpools of foam, recaptured, tossed again and turned over again...

Although solidly moored, the men were snatched away one after another, along with the masts and the funnels. I was waiting for the end: a disagreeable moment, damn it! But the tempest was making such an infernal din that I couldn't hear myself think, even by shouting, and I didn't have the idea of being scared. I only felt a great annoyance at missing an important rendezvous in Hong Kong.

How long that lasted, I can't say. At a given moment, lifted up by a wave more monstrous than the rest, I was rolled in its swirls, hurled like a cannonball in the midst of a firework display of white foam and red flashes, and I lost consciousness...

Whether that faint lasted for a week or only a matter of minutes, I can't say. When I came round, I had some trouble gathering my thoughts. Where was I? What, no longer dancing, no longer leaping, no longer tumbling? What tranquility, what calm after that frightful din!

Oh, my head! Oh my arms! Oh, my legs! I felt molded, demolished, broken all over, but the weather was delightful, the air smelled good, the waves were now like velvet paws caressing tenderly...so where was I?

Lying half in the water and half on pretty fine sand, I was able to raise myself up on my elbow and look round. "Land! An island!" Needless to say, I had been saved by a miracle; I finally perceived something other than water: a vast inlet framed by big rocks, with verdure behind, in the middle of which, tall coconut palms loomed up.

Saved, thank God! I savored the joy of finding myself out of danger, blissfully. My comrades, alas, had not had the same luck, and I couldn't see any wreckage of our ship, not even the smallest plank. The devouring ocean had not allowed a single fragment to reappear.

Yes, but I suddenly thought about savages. Damn! To escape a shipwreck only to fall into the hands of ferocious Kanaks wouldn't be pleasant! And I remembered a heap of stories of mariners shipwrecked on scantly inhabited shores, immediately and unceremoniously put on the spit, or fattened up in order to be served up one after another as the main dish of a great feast when the tribes got together and exchanged courtesies. I had to expect annoyances of that sort. Fortunately, I'm thin; I would have had a slight delay...

Those reflections introduced a hint of black into my satisfaction at finding myself out of the grip of the tempest. Crawling over the sand and in the water I was gazing anxiously at the shore when I suddenly heard cries and appeals uttered by strange voices, which even seemed to me to be savage and ferocious.

I turn around swiftly. It's a matter of not allowing myself to be devoured. I perceive indigenes running from rock to rock, gesticulating...

And I'm defenseless! They're hurtling toward me with an incredible rapidity. But they're on horseback, damn it! I hear the noise of hooves trotting over the shingle and through the first waves...*floc, floc...patapan, patapan...floc, floc...*

Here they are! I'm caught; they're hailing me in an unknown language... Let's at least try to mollify them, so they don't eat me immediately. I stand up, with a amiable smile. Why, there are only two of them, making enough noise for half a dozen....

Ah! Oh! Ah! Damn and double damn! I raise my arms in the air in amazement and fall to a sitting position in a pool of water, splashing my savages—*ploof!*—who jump in their turn, in an amazement similar to mine!

My savages, damn it, my local natives, aren't Kanaks, and they aren't negroes, Chinese or Malays... they aren't humans at all... or rather, they aren't all human. They're centaurs! Yes, centaurs of the classic species, those we know from fabulous accounts: mythological centaurs!

No, I'm not seeing things! I can really see them! I plunge my fists into my eyes and I rub hard... No, I'm not dreaming, they really are Centaurs, I tell you: CENTAURS! Creatures half-human and half-horse, as in fable, or what we took for fable. I've done my classes, I haven't forgotten what Greek legends say about the centaurs that lived somewhere in Thessaly and which troubled the wedding of Pirithous, king of the Lapiths...

Well, they're the same, exactly the same! Oh, my head! I'm ready to shout: "By Jupiter, would you care to go back into mythology right away!"

So, I raise my arms toward the heavens and wave them frantically. They do the same, raising their arms toward the heavens, just as bewildered as me, but as they each have four feet...four horse's feet and two human arms...they rear up on their hind legs, and manifest an amazement even greater than mine.

They utter exclamations in a sonorous language, which isn't Greek. I can divine perfectly well from the tone what they mean: *What is this extraordinary individual, this monster of an unknown species?*

Finally, after having rolled their round eyes for a long time, one of the centaurs bends down, catches me in his net and grabs me by the arms. I cling to him, he sets off, going back up the beach and pulling me into the rocks, on a slope that's a little too steep for my shipwrecked strength.

The other centaur follows, encouraging me, and pushing me at difficult spots, and we finally arrive outside the reefs on good soft warm sand. There I let myself drop in order to catch my breath and try to recover my spirits, which really isn't easy.

Soon I hear galloping around me, and I find myself surrounded by a band of centaurs and centauresses arrived from various directions, all uttering exclamations of astonishment and arguing animatedly.

*II. In which Captain Zephyrin, collected by natives
with our legs and two arms, progresses
from one surprise to another*

It's too much! The cyclone the hours and hours,
perhaps days, spent in my desperate situation, delivered
to all the caprices of the monstrous waves, finally running aground on that shore and, to finish it off, the appearance of the centaurs!

I nearly faint again—from fatigue, hunger and emotion, you understand! Doubtless they perceive it; a
centauress cuts through the crowd. She's holding some
sort of bottle in her hand. She…how shall I put it?…she
kneels down beside me and puts the bottle in my mouth,
while supporting my head with her other arm. She en-
courages me with words pronounced in a soft voice,
speech of which I can translate easily enough merely by
the intonation: *Come on, my friend, drink this for me;
it's good, very good, it will do you good!*

In fact, it is good; it's an excellent cordial, which
reanimates me and warms the blood in my veins. It's
more agreeable that being put on the spit, as I expected
to be.

My saviors number a dozen centaurs and
centauresses, plus a few little centaurs galloping alongside Papa and Mama.

No, they aren't Oceanian Kanaks, Kanak centaurs,
they're white, with a mat or slightly bronzed complex-
ion. The features are European, with fine brown beards.
There are blond ones too, however; among the three
centauresses that I came distinguish in the crowd, there's
one blonde—the one who gave me the cordial to drink.

And my centaurs are dressed; they aren't savages, I tell you. Naturally, they have bizarre costumes, very different from the national costumes with which I'm familiar—and God knows that I'm familiar with some on all five continents! They have simple enough tunics of a sort hanging down almost to their knees—their horse's knees, that is—attached by woolen belts dyed in bright colors.

The centauresses are wearing very similar tunics, but much more elaborately ornamented, with necklaces of glass beads around their necks. I can see that coquetry exists here too; the centauress who gave me something to drink has dangling metal brooches on her tunic, bracelets on her arms and even—how shall I put it?—on her horse's legs above the ankle...no, the fetlock.

There are fishers there and manual workers, I sense that by their rude and callused hands; there are also individuals of a more elevated status, doubtless bourgeois centaurs, who were out for a stroll on the beach, and came galloping with the others in order to bring aid to the castaway.

I'm questioned, interrogated, but I don't understand a word, although I can make a good guess.

How are you feeling now, poor unfortunate creature? Are you better? Come on, come as far as the houses over there...

I'm shown white and pink houses gleaming in the sunlight some distance away at the top of a hill. I nod my head as a sign of consent and I stand up, on legs that are still unsteady.

"Thank you very much, Messieurs et Mesdames," I say. "You're very kind. I'm feeling better and I'll go with you."

I distribute handshakes all round; they understand that I'm thanking them and look at one another with smiles of satisfaction.

The centaur fishers who found me first take the lead with their nets and baskets, in which strange fish are quivering, unknown in our cold northern waters. An obliging centaur, seeing that I'm still in some discomfort and limping, because of having been rolled over so many pebbles by the demented waves, and so brutally, picks me up and sits me astride s back, holding me firmly by the belt with one hand.

Equitation is not my forte, and I've known encountered simple horses elsewhere that have thrown me out of the saddle, sometimes to starboard and sometimes to port when it wasn't forwards or backwards, but this time I don't have to torment myself with reins or equilibrium, since my mount is holding me in place himself. All goes well and, transported by joy, I let myself go, crying: "Forward ho! Giddy up!"

Damn, that's not polite to my benefactors; I seem to be treating them like mere horses. Fortunately, my impoliteness passes unnoticed; they don't appear to hold it against me, and we go up the slopes at a gentle trot, the entirely troop chatting cheerfully.

What luck—the indigenes are good-natured, worthy people, mild and hospitable. Instead of putting the poor castaway on the spit and eating him with salt, they pick him up, comfort him and look after him. Let's go with the flow and see what happens.

Damn it! What a surprise, all the same. The country seems to be perfectly cultivated. Here are fields and gardens, well-maintained roads, even a signpost bearing an inscription in bizarre characters.

We travel rapidly, and I wouldn't have been able to follow my centaurs on foot. As we emerge from a little wood on to a plateau overlooking a vast horizon. I'm able to form an idea of the land to which the cyclone has brought me. The island—is it an island?—is large; as far as the eye can see I perceive a beautiful countryside, immense plains and undulating hills, between which rivers scintillate, snaking through meadows, fields and forests. I distinguish villages, and even larger agglomerations that must be towns.

At the farthest limit of the blue-tinted horizon, a chain of high mountains is outlined, blurred and disappearing into the clouds. Behind me is the sea, the immensity of the ocean, without a dot on the extreme blue line.

But I don't have time to linger in contemplation of the landscape; there are more people on the road or alongside it. I start on the rump of my horse—which is to say, the benevolent centaur who is carrying me. I can see metal shining, breastplates scintillating. What, soldiers? It's the cavalry...no, still centaurs, but soldiers, men of war.

To make sure that I'm not dreaming, and to see whether a sudden movement might wake me up, I let go of my centaur's tunic and let myself fall. I don't fall—the centaur catches me while trotting. I really am awake.

We arrive alongside the militia. They're sixty strong, all handsome fellows, young, strong and well-groomed, if I might put it thus. They wear steel helmets with bristling crests and breastplates of large steel plates, with short sleeves of chain-mail, from which muscular arms protrude. They're in the process of shooting at targets in a broad terrain bordered by the road. The target represents a white centaur with broad brown stripes on the hindquarters, like a zebra. The centaurs arrive at a gallop in groups of four, brandishing bows, and while galloping, release their arrow at the target. They seem to me to be skillful.

Suddenly, at the sight of me, the entire squadron suspends the exercise and they run to cluster around me, with cries and exclamations. A centaur officer, a golden chestnut with a handsome face, advances authoritatively and takes my arm in order to put me on the ground and examine me more easily.

The benevolent centaur serving as my mount explains:

"Be careful, don't break him! This strange animal is a trifle unwell. We found him on the beach; the sea cast him up... Yes, yes, he came out of the water. See, he's still all wet..."

That was what my mount said. The officer only replies with exclamations of astonishment, as we say "Sapristi!" or "Damn!"

He turns me around and around, his eyes wide; his men laugh, seemingly making fun of me.

"Pardon me, Officer," I say, in a vexed manner, "but I'm dying of hunger, and I'd like to go away with my rescuers, who'll doubtless take me to some inn."

He makes a gesture of command. His soldiers clear the road, line up and depart at a trot to resume their exercises. The arrows whistle toward the target again.

My rescuers address a few words of commiseration to me. One of them, a middle-aged centaur, a worthy bourgeois with a well-to-do air and a florid face, puts his hand to his mouth, which he opens wide. I understand.

"Hungry! Very hungry!" I said, energetically, opening my moth wide. "Horribly hungry!"

It was true. For how many days had I had nothing but splashes of sea-water over my body for my only nourishment. I didn't know, but my stomach was crying famine.

"Let's go to the houses—it's not far. Perhaps there's a restaurant...let's go, hup!" I say, impatiently

As we get closer to the houses, I perceive two or three centaurs with striped hindquarters like the zebra centaur painted on the target. But their type isn't the same, their features are different; my centaurs have proud aquiline noses like mine, in the European style; the noses of the zebra-striped centaur seems to me to be somewhat flattened, and their hue is more bronzed.

I hear a sound of wheels. So they have horses! I want to see...

No, they're carriages with arms, drawn by centaur laborers, vehicles laden with merchandise or raw materials, it seems to me—except for one, a rig of very bourgeois appearance. In a species of litter or wheeled chair, there is an aged centauress with white hair, wheeled by two centaurs, whose garments, of a particular cut, must be livery.

I also see a hirsute fellow passing, a ragged and dirty centaur covered in dust, as emaciated as an old cabhorse. His hands are bound and two uniformed centaurs are trotting behind him.

My friend points at him and explains. I understand. He's some vagabond, picked up by the centaur police, and doubtless being taken to prison.

III. A first glance over the city of the centaurs.
The Farrier.
Zephyrin makes the acquaintance of centaurian cuisine

We arrive in what is at least a big village, if not a town. I won't waste my time giving you a course in centaurian architecture. Only know that the houses seem to me to be similar to the Asiatic type. They're large white, pink, yellow or green cubes, very cheerful in appearance: only one upper floor, galleries on the ground floor, and immense arcades framing shops; on the upper floor, more galleries with glazed windows. Yes, they have windows, and even curtains behind them. I perceive that while trotting rapidly.

There are monuments. We traverse a square dominated by a huge edifice, which looks very much like a temple to me. The other side of the square is occupied by a low building without an upper story, from which a rumor of infantile voices is emerging. I recognize the rumor. I still don't know the centaurian language, but I can't be mistaken; it's something like: B, a, ba; B, e, be, B, o, bo!

The rumor stops, replaced by a racket of hooves striking the ground, and from all the doors of the edifice there's a stampede, a gallop of centaur foals, fillies to the right, colts to the left, who run, jump and race, snorting and shouting, with bursts of laughter. It's the end of the school day, as among us.

In the blink of an eye, we're surrounded. They've seen me, and here they are, under the legs of my escort, which is forced to come to a halt.

There are cries of astonishment that seem never-ending

"Oh what a funny animal!"

"Where did you find that?"

"Is it dangerous?"

"Let's see!"

"Are you giving it to us?"

"Look at its feet!"

"Can it walk?"

"Very polite, those little centaurs; a trifle bold, but polite nevertheless."

They have slender hindquarters and long thin legs, exactly like our colts. The majority are holding scrolls under their arms, which must be textbooks or notebooks. A few are bouncing balloons or carrying bags of marbles.

They come to feel and pinch my legs, manifesting a considerable astonishment. They would like to see me on the ground to discover whether I walk on two feet or four.

"We've arrived, haven't we?" I say.

The entire school bursts out laughing on hearing me speak. I make a sign to my mount, who helps me to jump down. There are cries of surprise.

"It stands upright on two feet! It can walk!"

At that moment, as my garments are still soaked with sea-water, I feel a slight chill and I sneeze.

A universal burst of laughter, accompanied by words that I have no difficulty translating as: *Bless You!*

The centaurs appear to me to be good people. My obliging friend takes me by the arm, and leads me to the entrance to the first street, saying something like: "You'll catch cold, poor little animal. Come this way and get warm."

There's a fire burning in the first house...but what's this I see on arrival?

The fire is that of a forge; the house is the workshop of a farrier. In front of the house, the man in question—no, the centaur-smith—is in the process of shoeing, not a horse, but a respectable lady centauress! Just as we see here, in our squares, especially on market days!

I hadn't yet noticed; my friends from the beach are all shod, all the centaurs have iron horseshoes, including the schoolchildren; that's audible when they gallop. The foot of the centauress is held by a centaur-workman; the centaur-smith sets the shoe on the hoof, applying the hot iron with tongs; he hammers and nails it...it reeks of burned horn...

It's done; the centauress lowers her foot and comes to look at me curiously before extending another.

I go into the smithy with two or three centaurs, and I'm taken to dry myself before the fire, which an apprentice stokes up.

The entire troop outside forms a compact crowd, the schoolboys in the front row trying to slip into the forge. They chat, they shout, they call out to me. Idlers intrigued by the crowd come trotting up and I see other curious individuals leaning over the upper galleries of the houses opposite.

It's hot in the forge. I've wrung out my jacket and waistcoat in order that they'll dry quickly. As I feel increasingly hungry, I click my teeth energetically to ask for some sort of nourishment

Understood! My obliging centaur signals to me with a nod of the head. *Let's go!*

He takes me by the arm and we depart, leaving the farrier to resume shoeing the centauress.

My protector takes me a short distance to a large house that has an inscription on the façade. We go into an immense hall in the center of which is a large table flanked with a few smaller ones in the corners. Good, it's an inn, and I'm in the dining rom.

But the tables are very high, at least a meter and a half. There are neither chairs nor benches, nothing but little leather cushions on the floor. A family is dining at one of the little tables: a centaur, a centauress and a little centaurin. I can see that the tables are adapted to their height.

A centaur in a white apron hastens forward and takes us to the big table. There are plates similar to ours of a kind of white faience and rounded glasses. But how am I to sit down at such a high table? Am I going to eat standing up? No, the waiter piles up the little cushion one atop another, and now my chin is level with the table.

In the meantime, my protector has given orders and the hotelier appears in person with the first dish. What can it be? When I consider those equine hindquarters I'm seized by suspicion regarding centaurian cuisine...and I'm a finicky eater! Too bad, it's pot luck. I'm too hungry.

Here's the dish on the table. What luck, an omelet! Was I stupid expecting to see hay arriving. It's a delicious omelet, with bacon and fine herbs, accompanied by a little pancake, doubtless the local bred.

I draw various bottles and jugs that I can see on the table toward me. There's water, very good, but I've drunk too much during my shipwreck. Here's a species of slightly sweet yellow wine that pleases me more.

When the omelet is expedited I make a sign that I'm still hungry. Good, the centaur hotelier responds that he's understood.

"Monsieur has chosen the menu," he says, or something like it, indicating my protector, the corpulent centaur.

Very well. Let's see what comes. Now that the edge has been taken off my hunger, what I feel most of all is curiosity. I don't have long to wait. A centaur-scullion and a centauress, who must be the hotelier's wife, bring me, one a fuming dish, the other a collection of plates of fruits and pots filled with something resembling compotes or kinds of jam.

Perfect! Let's see the main course! A large slice of roasted meat on a bed of unknown vegetables. Let's taste it. Not bad. Beef? Mutton? Rabbit? Elephant? Horse? What am I saying, horse? Among the centaurs, that's impossible. I can't guess; the taste is unfamiliar. My friend the stout centaur tells me what it is, but I can't grasp the word. Let's cut it short and get on to the fruits and preserves.

Suddenly, I slap my forehead. Damn it! I'm in a restaurant—how am I going to pay? I render myself culpable at that moment of the sin of bilking. I'm quite simply a crook. Quickly, I search my pockets; my money-clip has departed for the sea-bed. Ah, in my waistcoat: three copper coins, one of them English. I've eaten more than that! I continue searching. O joy! My wallet hadn't followed by money-clip; it's soaking wet, but that doesn't matter. I take out a hundred-franc bill and I hand it nobly to the centaur-innkeeper.

"Waiter, the bill," I say. "Pay, yourself!"

The centaur innkeeper looks at my banknote, turns it over and back; he shows it to his wife, who shows it to the waiter. My friend the stout centaur takes it and examines it. The blue image seems to interest them; they show one another the figures, which have two arms and two legs like me; then the innkeeper returns the bill to me, shaking his head.

"What, you're refusing a bill from the Banque de France, always well received throughout the five continents of the world? You're refusing?"

I add the three copper coins by way of a tip. It's pure generosity for, after all, damn it, I haven't eaten a hundred francs and thee sous' worth!

Things seem to be going badly. My innkeeper frowns and speak rapidly to his waiter

"Banque de France!" I say. "Me give a hundred francs! Good bill, me have no other money. Bill good everywhere!"

I talk in pidgin and shout, as if that might make my French more easily understood, but the worthy folk seem even more bewildered and refuse my bill more energetically.

The stout centaur intervenes, sketching a noble gesture. "Monsieur is my guest," he seems to be saying. And he also takes something out of a pocket in his tunic. It's a purse; he takes out a shiny coin.

"Very good!" says the innkeeper, picking up a rectangular slate on which he traces signs that must be numbers and presumably constitute my bill

I shake the hand of the stout centaur and I look at the gold coin. It's round, like ours; one on side there's a bearded head coiffed with a crown and on the other a centaur on foot, holding a sort of scepter in his right hand and a ball in the left...

Very curious. I collect the coins of all the continents; I have piastres, sapèques, yen, contos de reis...but not one of those.

"Bill good," I say to the stout centaur. "You change bill, give money to me..."

The centaur takes the bill, looks once again at the image, with interest, and puts it in his pocket carefully, but without giving me any change.

My lunch has cost me a hundred francs, life seems to be expensive here, I no longer have any but three sous for my entire fortune, so far from home! Damn! Let's eat copiously—I don't know whether I'll be able to dine this evening!"

And I finish the plate of meat that seemed so formidable, and stuff myself with compotes and jam.

*IV. Captain Zephyrin causes great excitement
in the streets of the city and the town hall.
A Family Reception*

There are still as many people in the street when I
come out of the restaurant. The entire city has come running to see the unknown biped cast up on the shore by
the tempest.

Where are we going now? The stout centaur makes
a speech of which I can only grasp one thing, which is
that he's inviting me to follow him. I'd like nothing better. Politeness obliges me to respond and thank him for
all his attentions.

"Where would I be without you, my dear benefactor?" I say to him. "You've nourished me; I've seen you
give a tip to the fishers who pulled me out of the water; I
consider you to be a worthy fellow of a centaur."

We continue on our way and we even find in the
street the two centaurs of the police force, in the process
of taking their vagabond into a large building with
barred windows.

My guide stops and has me precede him into the
courtyard of that forbidding edifice. What? Am I too
going to be considered a vagabond and lodged in the
prison with the other one?"

"Wait a minute! Wait a minute! I'm a honest travel-
er—without papers it's true, and with only three sous in
my pocket, but..."

A smile passes over the centaur's benevolent face.
He claps me on the shoulder. Reassured, I slap him cas-
ually on the rump.

"Let's go, me confident; you go ahead, me follow!" I say, resuming talking pidgin , which seems more intelligible to me in its simplicity.

No, the prison doesn't open for me; we turn into a gallery and traverse a vast room in which four young centaurs are working, sitting on little leather cushions, at high desks, like the restaurant table. They're writing with goose-quills on large pieces of paper or ledgers. My entrance has a considerable effect. The young individuals have seen me in the square, but they come to study me at closer range with ken interest.

My guide opens a door and we go into a second room, with walls garnished with pigeon-holes and tablets, like the first. A centaur of imposing appearance, who is working at a desk cluttered with stacks of paper, stands up. I guess that I must be in the office of the local mayor, in the presence of that official.

This one has not yet seen me; his eyes widen with surprise; he circles around me, makes me lift my head; he feels my knees, bends down to look at my shoes, and utters exclamations. My friend tells him about my arrival in the land, pointing through the window at the distant blue sea and the beach where the waves cast me up.

The official pushes cushions with his hoof and invites us to sit down. I'm forced to cross my legs in the Turkish fashion, which makes me seem very small beside my friend.

The official takes a large sheet of parchment, sharpens a goose-quill and looks at me gravely, pronouncing a few words in an interrogative tone. Doubtless he's asking me for my name and my forenames.

I respond immediately: "Zephyrin Canigousse, long-haul captain, domiciled in Bordeaux, Rue..."

The official makes a gesture.

"Forty-two and a half..."

Another gesture

"Traveling on business and at liberty here by virtue of misfortune at sea. You must have perceived the great tempest that raged a few days ago, a true cyclone, Monsieur le Maire! Can you imagine that my ship, the *Rose de Mai*, a fifteen-hundred-ton steamer, out of Bordeaux, as I told you, which set sail toward Indo-China, Siam, Tonkin, China and Japan, in order to..."

The mayor, his pen suspended over the paper, interrupts me.

"Am I going too quickly? You're not entirely satisfied? Wait, Monsieur le Maire. Permit me to write my name myself; I'm familiar with the orthography..."

I stand up and I borrow the mayor's pen. He's already scribbled a heap of distorted signs on his paper; underneath, in my finest calligraphy, I write my name and forenames, my address in Bordeaux and the name of my defunct ship.

"There," I say, returning the pen to him. "That will be more regular."

The mayor tries to read in his turn, and scratches his head. Then, taking up his pen again, he looks at me attentively and writes. It's evidently a description that he's recording; he gets up to come and verify the color of my eyes; then, in response to a summons, a centaur clerk arrives with a measuring-stick and measures me, like a conscript.. What vexes me is that they all seem to think me very small, with my one meter seventy-six. Well, I'm not like them, half a man planted on three-quarters of a horse.

Finally, it's done. The mayor shakes my friend's hand and deigns to clap me on the shoulder benevolently.

"Let's go," says my guide, drawing me away, after obligatory salutations.

Mechanically, I look for a tobacconist's shop in the street. My lunch is never complete if I can't light my little pipe afterwards. And I can feel it in my pocket—the sea hasn't taken it. Alas, there's no sign of tobacco in the street. We go past merchants of fruit and vegetables, a carpenter planning planks in his yard with his apprentices, a metalwork shop in which centaur craftsmen are hammering in cadence on the anvil, a bakery-patisserie in which centaur bakers in aprons are putting flat loaves in the oven, and a draper who is displaying his fabrics to lady centauresses, so interested that they don't see me passing by.

In sum, I glimpse most of the trades familiar to us, the equivalent of what one would find in a small provincial town. I even perceive a notary's office—at least, I suppose that's what it is; there are three centaur clerks scribbling on high desks and who get up tumultuously as I go past, in response to a summons from a young guttersnipe. Why, there's even a clockmaker. So the centaurs are no longer using the ancient clepsydra, or even the sundial. It's true that I remember seeing a clock in the mayor's office without paying any attention to it, by reason of having so many subjects to astonishment, amazement and stupefaction piled upon me since the morning.

In the clockmaker's window I perceive round clock-faces like ours, with the hour indicated by unknown signs. I count the signs; there are twenty of them. The centaurs employ decimal time.

Seeing me studying the clocks with interest, my friend rummages in his pocket and pulls out a large watch very similar to ours, except that a mobile part of the dial, rotating at will, is black, and serves to indicate the hours of darkness. I take out my chronometer in my turn, in order to have him admire it. Unfortunately, it has stopped; the sea-water has damaged it.

My friend seems very surprised, however.

That's curious; in fact, he seems quite intelligent, this little animal, he seems to be saying to himself.

But we stop in front of a large white house surrounded by a beautiful garden, and the centaur invites me to go in. At the sight of me, a centaur gardener, astounded, stops watering the flowers; a lady appears on the perron, and four or five centaurins of various ages run and trot around me, uttering exclamations of astonishment.

The benevolent centaur introduces me ceremoniously to the lady centauress, whom I deduce to be his wife, and he invites the children to be quiet. When he thinks that the children have contemplated me sufficiently, he makes a little speech and takes me into the house.

I understand that he said to me: "You are at home here, unfortunate castaway; you may install yourself; I shall be delighted to offer you hospitality."

The house isn't bad; evidently my hosts are well-to-do bourgeois. The benevolent centaur gives me a tour while his wife prepares refreshments in the garden. In the large and well-ventilated bedrooms, the beds appear to me to be bizarre; they're thick mats made of a soft vegetable tissue, like wool, with cushions piled on top. The centaurs lay their equine hindquarters on the mats and the upper body on the cushions.

The furniture seems expensive: large chests, massive tables, majestic wardrobes, everything shining under the polish. There's an absolute lack of chairs and armchairs, since the centaurs don't sit down in the same fashion as us.

There are family portraits in the drawing room, not life-sized, fortunately, for the walls wouldn't be sufficient. They are centaurs with grave and majestic expressions, important bourgeois, perhaps magistrates, and gracious centauresses or little centaurins with pretty faces.

We are summoned into the garden, where the young centaurins are waiting for me impatiently, sitting on the ground around a table laden with plates of cakes, cups and various utensils. I believe, God forgive me, that we're about to take tea!

Lady centauresses, probably neighbors who have come to see me, are laughing and chattering. Further introductions: "Charmed, Mesdames!"

My hostess hands me a cup of hot liquid. I taste it; it's tea—or very nearly. Not bad, with a dab of syrup instead of sugar.

They chat, and chat, and chat—about me, naturally, since I'm the great curiosity of the day. I tell the story of my shipwreck. I talk about Bordeaux, Paris, Europe... Those names mean nothing to the ladies; they don't understand, but they laugh. They tell me a host of things that I can scarcely grasp; they laugh, we laugh. The children play. The youngest, a beautiful blond and rosy-faced child, is one perpetual laugh.

"He's five years old," the centauress tells me, by raising five fingers.

"A charming child, Madame, and very strong for his age," I reply, trying to take him on my knees. Oof! I can't lift him: I forgot his young colt's hindquarters.

The time passes very agreeably. It's very comfortable in that house, with those worthy people. If only I had a cigar! But I haven't seen any centaur smoking.

The maid arrives—at least, I think it's the maid, a little centauress in a white tunic or apron—and hands a piece of paper to my host. He gets up urgently and makes a sign to me. There are visitors for me.

"I'm yours, my dear friend," I say, putting down my cup of tea. "All my apologies, Mesdames, very sorry to be quitting such charming company."

*V. A few centaur scholars want to classify
Captain Zephyrin in the family of monkeys.
The aforesaid Zephyrin's projects of vengeance*

In the drawing room, four individuals are waiting for us, grave middle-aged centaurs with gray beards and spectacles. At the sight of me they get up very quickly from their cushions and utter exclamations. By dint of hearing them repeatedly, my ears have already retained a few words of the centauran language.

"Extraordinary! Strange! A funny little beast!"

My host makes ceremonious introductions, and then embarks on explanations; the visitors take notebooks from their pockets with pencils of a sort, and scribble notes. They circle around me and bend down to examine me, studying my features in detail and the architecture of my body.

I understand that the messieurs are the scholars of the country, come to make a scientific study, from the viewpoint of natural history, of the strange animal deposited by the sea on the shore of their island.

One of the centaurs, a rather thin brown bay, draws my full-length portrait, facing and in profile, while holding a lively discussion with his colleagues. The messieurs don't all seem to be of the same opinion. Evidently, they don't know in what animal family to classify me.

My host goes to open one of the large cupboards in the drawing room. Why, it's a bookcase, full of books and scrolls of parchment. He takes out several large volumes, which he carries to the table. My four scientists lean over in order to riffle through them, and I stand on tiptoe in order to see.

There are pictures. Of course, it's something like an encyclopedia of natural history, with colored plates, a true masterpiece of centauran typography. I recognize a certain number of animals. One of the scientists, the most earnest, the one with the most badly-fitted cravat, pauses over an engraving and indicated it triumphantly to his colleagues, also indicating me with a gesture.

The wretch! The engraving is an illustration in which various species of monkeys are represented!

And he says—at least, I think I understand him to do so: "Look, Messieurs, that's exactly it; this bizarre individual, a stranger to our climes, belongs to the family of monkeys. He's a specimen of a previously-unknown species, a remarkable variety, which seems slightly superior to the others..."

The discussion becomes animated; with the illustration of monkeys in hand, I'm examined, turned back and forth, compared to the images...

I can't let that pass without protesting. Oh, no! So I become red-faced with annoyance.

"Damn it!" I cry "Double damn it! What do you take me for? I could call you utter asses, Messieurs Scholars! What, a monkey! Me, a variety of monkey? I'm a HUMAN, don't you know that, a HUMAN? And I'm more human that you are, who seem to me to the quite simply grafted on to donkeys!"

My centaur friend tries to calm me down. He doesn't accept the advice of the fake scholars and runs to fetch another volume, through which he riffles rapidly.

I perceive more illustrations. It's not natural history this time. Yes, it looks more like a mythology, a collection of fables and traditions. The depictions are bizarre.

There are centaurs and centauresses, but centaurs provided with huge wings, or holding various attributes. One is brandishing lightning, like Jupiter, another is causing the sun to rotate by means of a machine similar to a rotisserie, and there's also a centauress galloping through the clouds with a crescent moon on her head.

Having passed rapidly over a series of images representing a heap of monstrous creatures—fantastic dragons with claws and horns, chimerical mammoths, fabulous snakes, plesiosaurs and pterodactyls designed in a fashion that is perhaps somewhat fantasized—my friend finally stops, triumphantly at a page on which a being is depicted who, this time, is neither a monster nor a monkey, but purely and simply human, vaguely and imperfectly represented, but incontestably human, with two arms and two legs, a biped like you or me, with nothing equine about him.

The old scholar shrugs his shoulders. He doesn't want to let go. By his scornful expression, I understand perfectly well that he's objecting.

"Dreams! Fabulous traditions! Nursery tales, all that! Stories dating from the origins of the centaur race! Science, Messieurs, veritable science, which is only supported on positive realities, on verified facts, can't admit this ancient nonsense. These creatures, invented by poets, have never existed, and the animal phenomenon here present, in spite of the partial resemblance that he presents to a centaur, is nothing but a variety of the simian species, a superior monkey if you like, but a monkey!"

I interrupt him violently, and I brandish the book containing the portrait of the prehistoric man.

The old scientist puts his hand over my mouth.

"He speaks," he says, "but are the bizarre sounds that emerge from his lips really a language? There's no proof of that. Do you understand any of it? No! Me neither! And besides, look at the sheep"—he points at a species of sheep in the encyclopedia of natural history—"the sheep goes *baa, baa*...do you understand what the sheep is saying? The dog"—he points at a dog—"goes *woof, woof*; the cat"—he point to a cat—"goes *miaow, miaow*...do you understand? Can one claim in consequence that the cat, the dog and the sheep are talking? No, Messieurs! All that I can concede to you is that, at least at first sight, this monkey seems to be a remarkable and interesting species, but I shall reserve judgment until further and more serious study as to exactly how far the intelligence that it seems to possess might extend. For myself, I strongly doubt that it goes any further than pure and simple instinct..."

As he says that, the wretch palpates my head and taps my cranium with his finger in a disdainful fashion. I have a great deal of difficulty mastering my anger. Let's not forget that I'm on unknown shores, among people whose existence humans were still unable to suspect yesterday.

My friend the benevolent centaur tries to calm me down. The scientist who has drawn my portrait defends me ardently. He too brandishes the book in which the old popular traditions are collected.

"Who knows, Messieurs" he says, raising his hand, "whether some of these fables or traditions are quite simply memories altered to a greater or lesser degree since their origin? It's a defensible hypothesis. Let's not reject anything, and before reaching a conclusion, let's study this individual scientifically, let's research his intellect. Without any doubt, he differs from us considerably, to his disadvantage, but if, in the unexplored ocean that surrounds our homeland, there exists a distant land, a island, inhabited by a biped rather than a quadruped variety of the centauran race, what an immense discovery that would be, Messieurs!"

The old scholar shrugs his shoulders again in a scornful fashion, calls his colleague a poet and sticks the plate depicting monkeys under his nose.

My host palpates my knees and points to my feet while tapping his hoof.

"His feet are curious," he says. "Look, Messieurs, they're shod; I perceive the traces of nails..."

I've understood his mistake.

"But no," I say, "you're making an error, my dear friend."

And briskly, I take off my shoes, and I display my bare feet.

General astonishment; the centaurs are unfamiliar with footwear; their four equine feet have no need of it, and they thought that the leather of my ankle-boots was my personal and natural hide.

"They're hands!" they all cry.

"That's exactly what we see here," says the benevolent centaur, indicating the picture representing the prehistoric man.

"Pardon me," says the old scholar, my enemy, "I've made up my mind about this quadrumane; it's entirely and definitively a monkey."

One of the messieurs nods his head in approval, while the other two, along with my friend, respond with signs of negation.

The discussion becomes heated, while I dart furious glances at my two enemies. The wretches! To classify me among the monkeys—me, Zephyrin Canigousse, long-haul captain, baccalaureate in letters...or almost, as I seem to remember that I was refused...

Against the two imbeciles who believe me to be a monkey I have three friends to defend my cause. For them, I'm the representative of an unknown race, intermediate between the centaur, the king of creation, and the animals.

Suddenly, my friend the stout centaur slaps his forehead. He rummages in his pocket and brings out my hundred-franc banknote, which he holds out to my enemies victoriously.

"Look!" he seems to be saying. "The pictures on this blue paper prove that the castaway here present isn't a unique individual. He's a specimen of a race living somewhere—I don't know where—on an island in the ocean, a race presenting certain indications of intelligence, since it seems to know the Arts, as this image demonstrates, which might perhaps represent the castaway's family, his wife and children, because it seems quite precious to him."

The others continue to shake their heads. They're not convinced. Now they seem to be interrogating my host as to what he intends to do with me. It appears that I belong to him; he's paid a certain sum to the fishers that picked me up on the beach like flotsam. He shows them the bedroom where he has offered me hospitality, and he puts his hand on my head as a sign of protection. Worthy friend!

The others emit different opinions. One of them makes a proposal, which he explains at length. I don't grasp it very well. Finally, he takes a pencil and draws some kind of plan on a piece of paper.

Ah! Damn! I've understood…it's a cage that he's drawing! The rogue is proposing to my host that he put me in a cage and exhibit me like a curious beast. The villain! I leap up. I'm on the point of slapping him in the face...but he's too tall, for one thing, and for another, with a single blow of the hoof, a kick, he could send me flying to the other end of the room...

Let's contain ourselves; the situation isn't looking very god for me, in spite of the support of the benevolent centaur, but with prudence and energy, one can fight, one can get out of it...

I don't allow myself to be beaten. And now, in fact, a vast project is germinating in my mind that ought to give me glory and fortune. In sum, such as I am, a poor defenseless castaway, alone and naked, with three sous in my pocket, I'm a great man! I've discovered a sixth continent of the world, absolutely unsuspected before, a large island, a continent inhabited by a race of centaurs—a race that once existed in Europe, as ancient traditions attest, which are treated as fables in colleges, a race vanished as a consequence of cataclysms mentioned vaguely by history or legends.

Well, I've rediscovered them, those fabulous centaurs! I have them, they exist at a point on the globe where I, the first of the human race, have set my foot! It's an immense discovery!

If I can return to Bordeaux with only two living and talking specimens of the centauran race, I'll become an illustrious navigator, a new Christopher Columbus, and I'll pass under triumphal arches, and all the Academies in the world will weave crowns for me...

And I'll exhibit my two centaurs in a cage similar to the one that my enemy has just designed for my intention...one franc, per person, fifty centimes for children, twenty-five for unranked military personnel...

And I'll make a dazzling fortune rapidly, millions heaped upon on millions in my coffers; I'll build myself an enormous and splendid mansion at the mouth of the

Gironde, in order to get a good view of the ships passing by…I'll buy land, vineyards, two or three great vintages to show off my cellar...

That's it! That's what I'll do! And the two centaurs that I'll take to Europe, to have them exhibited in a fine, strong case, well, they're the two scientists, my enemies, who take me for a monkey!

VI. Excursions and distractions
with the Kapalouia family

For two months I've been living with my protector, the stout centaur, treated very amiably—I might almost say considered as one of the family. I go out, I see society, I'm taken on excursions, I dine in town.

My friend is a worthy centaur; thanks to him I have every facility for studying the country and its inhabitants, their customs and mores. Thus, I'm collecting notions and information regarding the race, with a view to the account of the voyage I shall write when I return to my homeland, for I have my idea, on the quiet, and I'm gradually ripening the project that will give me glory fortune and revenge.

I learn the centauran language; it's almost easy when one knows Basque, the oldest language in the world, which was spoken long before Adam and Eve.

My friend's name is Monsieur Kapalouia, a majestic name that goes well with his corpulence and yet which means if I'm not mistaken, "little cherry." His wife answers to the pretty name of Azuli, which can be translated as "blue moonlight seen through dark clouds." What fine things can be expressed in so few syllables!

They have five children, three centaurins and two centaurines. Mademoiselle Rakif, or "beautiful star," is fifteen years old, a lovely centaurine already engaged to an officer, Monsieur Pilo-pilo, or "cabbage heart," who commands a garrison of eighty centaur archers, the ones I saw shooting at targets on the day of my arrival. And, in fact, I recall that on that day, Captain Pilo-pilo was

extremely polite to Monsieur Kapalouia, his future father-in-law.

Then come two boys, Karfalo and Topa—
"rainbow" and "light pastry"—twelve and ten years old,
brown bays, both quite pleasant although restive and
turbulent. Then Mademoiselle Mirako, or "little stork,"
nine years old, and Glouglou, "rat-whiskers," five and a
half, a charming, expansive child, always singing and
capering, who is already as tall as me, on the slender
legs of a young colt.

The centaur Kapalouia is rich; he's the owner of
several vast farms in the vicinity of Birka—I've forgotten to tell you that the place in which I landed is called
Birka. It's a small town of three thousand souls, built on
the shady banks of a river that ours into the sea a short
distance from the beach where I as picked up.

Monsieur Kapalouia has already taken me to visit
his farms, often during trips to the country with his entire family. Those instructive excursions delight me; I
study centauran agriculture and collects documents on
the customs and mores and the arts and métiers of the
centaurs; but they're also very tiring for me. I only have
two short legs—remember that the messieurs the centaurs are much more liberally endowed by nature. They
possess four legs; they trot, they gallop, they swallow up
kilometer after kilometer without thinking about it, while
I can scarcely keep up with the little ones when they only go at walking pace. As soon as they start to trot, I'm
outdistanced.

That still applies even when the journey is short.
There's a farm five or six kilometers away to which we
often go, but when it's a matter of covering four or five
leagues and as many on the return journey, that seems
very hard to me.

In spite of their advanced state of civilization, the centaurs are ignorant of all our means of locomotion: railways, automobiles, diligences and omnibuses. That's understandable. They have no need of all that, with their equine legs they can disdain steam-engines. The charm and poetry of their countryside aren't spoiled by those infernal vehicles running through clouds of dust or plumes of smoke, spreading the odor of coal and oil everywhere.

Through the cultivated plains or grassy meadows there are good tranquil roads on which no roaring, bellowing or honking vehicles roll; families can trot here at their ease and allow little centaurins of young age run and skip without any fear. No other vehicles exist except carriages drawn by hand, for excessively heavy loads, or sedan-chairs of a sort for aged or infirm centaurs.

Those worthy centaurs! It is quite amusing to see them, during the rainy season—which lasts for three or four weeks—going out under immense umbrellas and trying to shield their hindquarters, and little centaurins with hoods galloping and splashing through the puddles.

In the sunshine, our family excursions are very cheerful, the centaurins galloping around with joyful hearts. They play countless tricks on me, trotting and jostling around me. Sometimes Mademoiselle Little Stork and Monsieur Light Pastry each take one of my arms and lift me up during a gallop through the fields, making me jump over bushes and ditches. I laugh at first, and then get annoyed.

"Let me go, you young rascals—you'll dislocate my arms, damn it!"

"Forward!" they cry "Be good, you'll jump with us, Monsieur Zephyrin, you'll jump!"

"Please stop! I'm going to lose my shoes in the brushwood...I need to hang to my shoes! Are you going to make me another pair when I no longer have them? You don't need shoes...cobblers are unknown in your country; when your horseshoes are worn you go to a farrier. And besides which, you're taking my breath away, double damn it!"

"Dub...doubled..." the little centaurin Rat-whiskers tries to repeat.

"Get iron shoes yourself, Monsieur Zephyrin," said Mademoiselle Little Stork, "It's much more convenient. Try it—I'll take you to our farrier, who's very skillful...

I'm exhausted by that steeplechase with my little centaurins.

"Me worn out," I say to my friend Kapalouia, in the centauran language, spoken slightly pidgin-fashion. "You, not so fast!"

I daren't propose that he take me on his back, as he did during my rescue; his dignity as an important centaur, a notable bourgeois, forbids him absolutely from carrying any kind of parcel.

"Poor Zephyrin!" said Kapalouia. "What if you were to ride an ox?"

I've forgotten to tell you that there are cattle, or buffaloes, of a sort in their pastures, animals bred for milk, for meat or for laboring the fields.

"Oxen too slow," I say. "Oh, if only you had a donkey..."

"Donkey?"

Kapalouia looks at me interrogatively. I don't understand the language well enough to launch into a description, but I make "hee haw, hee haw" noises.

Kapalouia repeats: "Hee haw," but without it signifying anything to his mind; our good, worthy and likeable donkey is unknown among the centaurs. What a pity!

*VII. Captain Zephyrin refuses a little operation,
although it would allow him to avoid many humiliations*

What also annoys me is that my friend Kapalouia often looks at me with an air of profound commiseration, as if to say "Poor Zephyrin!"—which eventually becomes humiliating. He circles around me, examines me, and shakes his head sadly.

Evidently, he considers me to be a poor cripple because I don't have the equine hindquarters and four legs of centaurs.

Without a doubt, that's regrettable. Until disembarking here, I had never thought of complaining about it, but I'm obliged to agree that the centaurs, those human quadrupeds, can lay claim to a real superiority over the simple two-legged humans that we are.

What facility that conformation gives them from the point of view of communications! What enormous advantages over poor bipeds, obliged to employ all sorts of means in order not to trail painfully an interminably on their two poor little feet, to torture the mind in order to find a heap of inventions designed to remedy the unfortunate motor weakness of legs.

Whereas the centaurs laugh at distances, and make mock of the cabs and omnibuses into which we pile as soon as we have three kilometers to travel! For them, three kilometers is three minutes of tranquil healthy exercise. They have never had any need to invent the locomotive, the bicycle, the automobile and their airplane!

Decidedly, on reflection, I recognize that my friend the centaur Kapalouia is right; we are an inferior race. The superman is the centaur.

That humiliates me and puts me in a bad mood. The day after one of our little excursions, Kapalouia comes into my bedroom as I'm resting , fatigued by the kilometers traveled, even though my friends walked with a careful slowness, stopping continually to wait for me.

"My dear Zephyrin," the benevolent centaur says to me, "come downstairs with me for a minute; I have something to show you."

I follow him, painfully, for I'm still aching. Kapalouia is quicker than me in getting to the ground floor; in spite of their equine conformation, the centaurs descend their staircases, which are broad and not very steep, very well. The children gallop up and down the all day long, from the top of the house to the bottom.

"What is it that you want to show me?" I ask.

"Well," says the worthy Kapalouia, "I've noticed that you're chagrined by not being like us—don't deny it, it's not worth the trouble. As I like you a lot, that troubles me as much as you. Well, let's console ourselves, perhaps there's a means of arranging things..."

"How's that?" I say, nonplussed.

"Yes, yes, I can understand it perfectly; if I were in your situation I'd bemoan not being made like everyone else and I'd also be very humiliated. People look at you and feel sorry for you; that general commiseration can't be agreeable to your pride, I understand that. Everywhere you go people say: *Poor fellow! Look how he's built! Don't talk to me about it, it breaks my heart! Poor devil, with his two little legs! Funny conformation, all the same! He's nailed to the ground, so to speak, by that infirmity! And how ugly they are, those two excuses for legs...*"

"Yes, yes, me have heard all that often..."

"And you're not content! Well, I don't want you to suffer any more from those disadvantages, my fear friend; we're going to arrange all that by means of a little operation."

"What?" I say, surprised and a little frightened.

"Yes, it's fundamentally quite simple. What is it necessary to do? Get rid of those two short legs, which render you such scant services, and replace them with…"

"Oh, no! I'm fond of me two legs. I don't want to have them cut off!"

"Child! You don't know the skill of our surgeons! The art of surgery has made so much progress in our epoch! We have farrier-surgeons who sometimes have to risk very difficult operations after accidents, which work out admirably. Here, do you remember the old beggar we encountered last week?"

I do indeed remember a mendicant centaur on a road, whose singular appearance had struck me. He was advancing with his satchel on his back, his hindquarters under a ragged mantle, with an old scarecrow hat on his head, his forelegs hammering the ground with bizarre clip-clop. One looking at him more closely I perceived that his forelegs were crudely carved out of wood.

"Yes," I say, "me saw him."

"Well, that unfortunate, for want of resources, had wooden legs made for him by a village carpenter, but better ones can be found; we have people here who work artistically, and if you want, I wouldn't even hesitate, for you, to bring a surgeon from the capital. Once rid of those paltry and almost useless legs, we'll unite you with well-carved hindquarters, four ingeniously articulated legs that will walk I guarantee it! It will be a fine operation, and you'll no longer be a cripple, an object of pity for everyone..."

"Absolutely not! Definitely not! I don't want to; I like my own legs! Quite possibly, they're inferior in quality, but I've had them for such a long time! I'm used to them..."

"You're making a mistake—think of the advantages you're disdaining..."

"Me not disdaining, me recognize the advantages, but me afraid..."

"Afraid of what?"

"The operation."

"Trivial! It'll be over so quickly, and you'll be so content afterwards. Come on, say yes..."

"No, no! Me thank you, but beg you not to insist. I want to go back to my homeland with my own legs, as I left..."

"Go back to your homeland? But how? I'd like to believe that your homeland exists, since you affirm it and you've already tried to describe it to me...but it astonishes me all the same; our scholars have never heard mention of it. The universe consists of our homeland, completely surrounded by the sea with a few little inhabited islands scattered here and there, but there's nothing else on the entire surface of the globe. I have to tell you that we don't much like navigation; we have boats on the sea, but small, light fishing-boats, whereas you talk about big ships in your homeland. Anyway, I'll admit that you're not exaggerating... So be it, your homeland exists, there are other individuals of your race, populations of poor two-legged cripples like you; I'll even consent to that, since you wish it...but even sup- posing that you could go back there..."

"But I have every intention of doing so," I say.

"Ingrate! Are you not well off here, with us, among us, the centauran people, who have reached the summit of civilization? Anyway, so be it, supposing that you could return to your homeland, wouldn't you be very glad to return with an immense superiority over your brethren, to disembark among them proudly, with the hindquarters and four legs of a centaur? And, who knows, perhaps bringing them the idea of an immense progress? Think about it! Come on, yield to the temptation, let me summon the surgeon…only a consultation; he'll explain the matter better than me. It won't commit you to anything—a simple consultation!"

"Me thank you very much, but all the same, me content with my two legs. You, friend Kapalouia, not bring your farrier; me not want it."

"You're causing me pain, but I don't want to annoy you. Madame my wife had thought of having it done while you were asleep. One morning you'd have had the joyful surprise of finding yourself rid of your poor little legs…oh, how glad you would have been! It was a good idea, it would have avoided the annoyance of preparations…but I didn't think I ought to adopt that course; your legs are your own, and I would have had scruples about disposing of them without your consent, even with the certainty of acting for your own good."

"Thank you, my dear Kapalouia," I said, pressing his hands affectionately.

"And then again, I must say that your refusal only astonishes me a little; I half-expected it. You don't know the skill of our surgeons, and you have the weakness of being fond of your useless little legs; you're afraid of not being able to make appropriate use of the artificial legs that would be fabricated for you…so I expected..."

"I'll have to resign myself, then."

"Not at all! There's another means; there's something else we can try, at least to save appearances and avoid perpetual humiliations..."

"Me not understand what you mean."

"You'll understand soon! You'll see... Here, this is what I wanted to show you."

The good centaur opened the door of the room in which Madame Kapalouia's portable chair was kept.

"Come on! What do you say now?"

"What's that? A wooden horse?"

Alongside the portable chair he showed me a kind of painted wooden horse, quite well carved, but incomplete—which is to say deprived of a head and neck.

"You have horses on your island, then?" I exclaimed. "You told me before that you didn't..."

"And you wanted to make me believed that there exists in your homeland a species of animals resembling us somewhat in the lower half of the body...you must be exaggerating the resemblance. I repeat to you that we don't have that here, and I'll add that what you say is rather wounding for us..."

"Why?"

"We'd resemble animals, for, according to you, those horses are simple animals domesticated by you. I believe that's a little invention of your imagination...for you gallop madly into fantasy when you tell stories about your homeland, admit it! Anyway, you get confused in your stories; you've also talked to us about steam engines, which are only simple clouds...how do you expect me to believe you? Admit, then, that your horses and are pure allegories, fictions of poets who have extracted from ancient traditions a vague idea of the centaur, and, aspiring to the true beauty, superiority and perfection that's forbidden to you...but let's get back to my proposal. You see this machine..."

"Yes, that..."

"Stop there! It's not a horse, it's half of the body of a wooden centaur, a toy that was given to my daughter Rakif to amuse her, a big doll that she dressed and undressed and rolled around the garden."

"Oh, very well..."

"I've removed the upper part; nothing any longer remains but the hindquarters and he legs."

"That's what made me mistake the object for a..."

"Yes, yes...and I propose to attach it to you at the waist as a complement."

"I'd have six legs."

"That's true. I'm also going to take off the forelegs. So, we attach to your waist these wooden hindquarters—they're very light, and there are little castors on the feet. We drape that decently, and you'll have the appearance of a true centaur, or very nearly—not very tall, undoubtedly, not very favored by nature, but, in sum, a centaur. With that, people won't look at you in the street like a curious animal, they won't pay too much attention to your imperfections, and the street-urchins will no longer follow you and trot around you..."

I wanted to raise objections. Dragging that machine behind me would be a rather cumbersome disguise, and heavy, in spite of the castors. What a hindrance! But I sense that an overly abrupt refused might hurt the feelings of my good friend Kapalouia, who, after all, is only seeking to make himself agreeable to me with his idea of a operation or his wooden centaur.

Oh, it's time to leave this country! It's necessary to try to advance as much as possible the execution of my project of flight, not alone, but abducting at least two well-chosen specimens of the centauran species—which is to say, the two scientists, my enemies.

However, a reflection that I made inclined me to accept Kapalouia's proposal, for form's sake. That was that, in his generosity, in his ardor to do me good, he might end up acceding to the idea of his wife, the excellent Madame Azuli, and summon the farrier-surgeon while I was asleep.

"It's agreed," I say, "except that, in order to accustom myself to dragging it behind me, I'll practice for some time in the garden."

"Good, you're becoming reasonable."

VIII. The Scientists Bibouf and Galibou.
Further humiliations for the quadrumane Zephyrin

You can imagine that I don't want to live entirely as a parasite in the home of my friend Kapalouia. Lodged, nourished, cared for, taken on excursions, clad and glorified by artificial hindquarters, I am literally overwhelmed with benefits.

Kapalouia has had garments tailored for me, in order to spare my poor castaway's wardrobe. An old grayhaired tailor has copied my jacket and trousers as well as he could. Footwear posed a greater difficulty; he ended up addressing himself to a bookbinder who fabricated leather slipcases of a sort for me, which I lost at every step, and I had to be a cobbler myself in order to reshape them into something more closely resembling shoes.

As I desire in my turn to render some services to those worthy centaurs, for whom I feel an ardent amity, I have started giving French and English lessons to the children, which cannot fail to be very useful to them one day when, thanks to me, communications have been established between the human and centauran societies, when I have reattached Centaur Island to the rest of the world.

In any case, those lessons have a role to play in my plan, my famous departure plan, for as well as teaching French to the little Kapalouias, I'm also teaching it to my two enemies, Messieurs Bibouf—"Sunstroke" in our language—and Galibou, or "Red Parrot," the two scientists who only want to see me as a slightly improved monkey.

Very shrewdly, I have thus found a means of entering into a continuous relationship with them; gradually, I am insinuating myself into their confidence and bringing them to the desired point. That is making progress; you'll soon see how rapidly.

For their part, they're delighted. Those French lessons provide them with an ideal means of studying my intelligence, my instincts, my tastes and my habits. We are, therefore, living on excellent terms. I'm making sufficiently rapid progress in the centauran language; I'm striving to get as much information as possible out of my two enemies regarding the race, many curious and picturesque notes about its life and mores, for the relation of my voyage.

One day, as I am about to give those messieurs their French lesson, my friend Kapalouia hands me a scroll of paper.

"Here," he says, "read this, if you can; it's this morning's newspaper, and there's mention of you..."

I've forgotten to tell you that the centaurs, like us, have newspapers of a sort, not daily, but appearing once a week or every ten days, occupied with literature and serious news, not political chatter.

I'm almost beginning to know how to read; with patience and attention I arrive at understanding.

"Look, there in that column," Kapalouia tells me, in order that I won't waste my time searching the paper.

Indeed, it does concern me. It's a kind of report to a scientific academy by Messieurs Bibouf and Galibou, my two pupils and enemies.

And this is what I read:

To the learned and illustrious Academy of Sciences of Zinor, greetings and reverence!

Bibouf and Galibou, humble disciples, are sending the present communication with regard to an extremely interesting and curious individual recently fished up on the beach of Birka, on to which the waves of the sea had cast it, after a big storm.

Thanks to the kindness of Monsieur Kapalouia, who has received him in his house, we have had every facility to study the aforementioned extraordinary animal, and to enable us to render a full account of its real physical nature, its intelligence and its mores. After two months of serious study, examinations and comparisons with other species in the animal kingdom, we believe that we are sufficiently enlightened on the subject today to determine its zoological classification.

Description of the individual:

(I have a strong desire to pass over the description; my two enemies Bibouf and Galibou do not find me very handsome, but I can pay them back immediately, when I've told you that Bibouf had a flat face, a snub nose, not much hair, a long and ill-combed beard, while Galibou, by contrast, projected ten centimeters in front of a face like a blade a nose like the prow of an ironclad ship, mounted by two large round spectacles, masking slightly squinting eyes. Thus they are photographed; I shall say no more in order not to be suspected of animosity...)

Description of the individual, etc. etc. Five feet four inches, oval face, dolichocephalic head of mediocre cranial capacity, low forehead, prominent cheekbones, nose strongly aquiline, slanting eyes, green irises of cunning expression..., etc.

Facial angle too distant from the line characteristic of the centauran race for the individual to be related to us, although also rather distant from the facial angle of the great apes.

A vague resemblance to the centauran race can be observed in the conformation of the torso, the breast and shoulders, but that resemblance, which might seem striking to a superficial observer, cannot stand up to an attentive examination.

Torso short, arms thin and long, hands long and fingers loose, indicating a certain dexterity... Legs short and heavy, devoid of elegance and more similar to arms than true legs...

Instead of feet designed to receive iron shoes, the individual's legs are terminated by veritable hands, with articulated and gripping fingers, which is the most marked characteristic of the simian race, and would be sufficient to determine its relationship with the great apes even if there were not other indications to lead us to that conclusion.

In spite of all our invitations, even promising recompenses that ought to flatter its gluttony, the creature in question has always refused to climb trees, although its conformation would lend itself to that admirably. Its penchant for dissimulation as always retained it at the moment of allowing us to see its aptitudes.

Paleontology has discovered in the strata of the age immediately preceding the appearance of centaurs on earth skulls and fragments of the skeletons of great apes that must have been very similar to the individual we are studying. It would be very interesting to be able to compare its skeleton with those of some of the great apes in question reconstituted in the Museum in the capital.

We hope, in the interests of science, that circumstances will one day permit that comparison, and that it will be given to us to see, thanks to the munificence of Monsieur Kapalouia, the individual in question carefully naturalized in a glass case alongside those ancient counterparts.

I choked with anger on reading those lines, which Monsieur Kapalouia so obligingly placed before my eyes, striving to explain the difficult words and turns of phrase.

They had certainly classified me, those two fake scientists, pretentious individuals, complete asses rather than centaurs! Not content with making me a monkey, they were proposing quite simply to have me stuffed, like a curious ad rare animal, and putting me in a glass case in the Museum with a nice label. And for that they were making an appeal to the munificence of the good Kapalouia, to whom I belonged as a domestic animal!

Kapalouia saw my fury, which he mistook for dread.

"Don't worry, my dear little fellow, I won't give you to the Museum. Bibouf and Galibou are two schemers, who would be charmed to make a name in science by causing you grave displeasures, but I won't lend myself to their whim.

"Thank you, excellent Kapalouia, my benefactor; I can see that you're very sincerely my friend. You won't have me stuffed, even richly!"

"Never! When I think that they dare to propose such things, when you've been so obliging toward them…"

"Let's see the rest," I said picking up the newspaper again.

In spite of the feeble capacity of its cranial cavity, the individual we are studying appears to be capable of assembling a few simple ideas and expressing them in articulated sounds, in a voice fairly similar to the centauran voice.

It has a language of which, after a few months of patient study, we have succeeded in constituting the commencement of a dictionary and a sketch of the grammar, which she shall submit to the Academy imminently. That faculty of speech is, above all, what differentiates it from the apes that we know, but other animal species also have a sort of language; parrots and other birds talk, and give the impression while chattering at one another of expressing ideas...

How do we know whether the apes of the prehistoric era might not also have possessed speech? How can we be sure that they were not also capable of coordinating and expressing ideas?

In conclusion, we have no hesitation in placing the individual in question in the class of the superior great apes. It is a vertebrate mammal of the order of Quadrumanes, of an unknown family...

It originates from some tiny island lost in the immensity of the ocean that surrounds us. That little island is not a sterile rock, it is fertile ground; plants and trees fairly similar to our own are encountered here, doubtless by courtesy of seeds transported the wind and rots cast up there by the waves.

It has told us that it answers to the name of Zephyrin, difficult of orthography in our language.

The members of Zephyrin's species live in troops in fairly large villages, of which the principal one is named Bordo or Pary, for Zephyrin sometimes gives it one of those two names and sometimes the other. They know a few arts and métiers and even possess a few embryonic sciences. They are able to weave garments, cook their aliments and build huts.

Their confirmation and their four gripping hands, like those of apes, indicate sufficiently that they are es-

sentially climbers, which must establish their dwellings in the branches at the top of trees, for their security. That must, in fact, be the sole means for them to shelter themselves from the enterprises of ferocious beasts, since the weakness of their forearms prohibits them from fighting, just as their inaptitude in running prevents them from finding their salvation in flight in case of attack...etc.

Doubtless the search for the island where these quadrumanes live would present a scientific interest, especially from the viewpoint of natural history, but success appears to us to be so uncertain, and the result would offer such poor compensation for the risks, the enormous dangers and the immense expense, that we would not dare propose such an expedition. In that matter, as in all others on all others, it is to the luminaries of the Academy that the undersigned respectfully defer.

Bibouf. Galibou.

That took up six columns in the newspaper, plus a column and a half of notes. I had had enough; I shrugged my shoulders, laughing, determined to conceal the anger whipped up in me by all that ignominious rubbish.

"You aren't holding it against them," Kapalouia said to me. "I'm delighted by that; it proves that your nature is better than they suppose. I knew it!"

"No, I don't hold it against them, but I intend to show them that they're grossly mistaken, that they're floundering and splashing around, plunged neck-deep in error, all the way up to their spectacles."

Patience, patience! The plan was ripening that was to get me away from Centaur Island, a pleasant and charming land, I recognized, inhabited by worthy people like my friend Kapalouia—but where scientists dare to

205

propose to have me stuffed for the Museum in the capital,

I shall not be stuffed; I shall not ornament their Museum. On the contrary; I shall find a means of returning to my homeland and I shall disembark gloriously in Bordeaux, with my two insulters, the centaurs Bibouf and Galibou, in a good solid cage.

IX. In which Captain Zephyrin begins his preparations
for escape with the complication of abduction,
in order to bring back a few souvenirs of the land

Following my plan, I showed myself increasingly gracious with my two enemies, Bibouf and Galibou. I continued to teach them French and English, and even Basque. They continued taking notes in my regard, probably as malevolent as the earlier ones.

In addition to languages, still following my plan, I informed them on the subject of the sciences, and I spoke to them above all about everything relating to navigation.

Sailing is not the centaurs' forte, as I have already said, nature not having shaped for traveling the sea in boats, where they would be very cumbersome. It is for that reason that in all their travels over the oceans, humans, before me, had never found themselves face to face with those improbable and fabulous beings, considered by us to be a mythological chimera. It is for that reason, too, that they thought the universe limited to their island.

The centaurs did however, have boats for coastal fishing. We often directed our excursions toward the little port, and I examined those boats attentively. Not bad at all, those boats, large and rounded, and strongly-built. Although poor mariners, the centaurs are good carpenters, ingenious with rigging.

I rubbed my hands. On one of those boats, which held solidly at sea, I would dare to launch myself toward the distant horizon, in a north-easterly direction, the route to know lands, to Europe and the fatherland.

Alone, since there was no means of doing otherwise, I would confront all the dangers of the hostile regions.

But I don't want to go back alone; I want to return to Bordeaux with the two centaur scientists, my enemies. The difficulties are unimportant, great as they might be; I shall do it! I need a complete triumph, or nothing at all! A triumphant return to Bordeaux, or Bibouf and Galibou can have me stuffed for the Museum, if they so wish!

In the port, therefore, I talked about sailing with Bibouf and Galibou, who continued to study me covertly and make mental notes concerning me.

"Look at that large boat, then, illustrious Bibouf," I said to him. "Not built for racing, it would be beaten hollow at the regattas of Arcachon. You don't know Arcachon?"

"Is that one of your brothers?" asked Bibouf.

"No, I'll explain...later, when we reach Bordeaux. Look at that boat: it's solid, it travels well over the waves...I'd like to make an excursion on it."

"I understand an excursion at sea," said Galibou, "but for fishing, for science, to study curious fish..."

"Well, I said, "why not go to spend an hour or two off the coast of one of those islets out there?"

"It's just that I get sea-sick as soon as I set foot on a boat, and Bibouf too. In sum, though, for science, one might risk a little sickness—not so, my dear Bibouf?"

Bibouf nodded his head.

I also talked about it to Kapalouia, and everything was arranged in accordance with my desires. A few excursions were organized. A large boat with a deck was put at our disposal, containing a large room in its bulbous hull for the three centaurs who ordinarily manned it.

It could be steered from a sort of elevated poop, where the tiller commanding the rudder was located, quite simple and ingeniously organized. Usually, two centaur sailors fished while the captain, nonchalantly lying down, maneuvered his vessel without difficulty or fatigue.

After a few courses of study, the maneuvering would go perfectly. We've seen better than that in races at Arcachon in a strong breeze.

Splendid weather favored the first excursion with the Kapalouia family. How pleasant it was on that blue sea, before that sunlit coast, with those worthy centaurs! My heart dilated in my breast. It would not have taken much for my resolution to weaken, and I would have renounced flight, resigning myself to live on that truly delightful island, if the humiliating idea had not returned to me that, among the good centaurs, agile and galloping, with my short and feeble legs, I was nothing but a kind of cripple, almost nailed to the ground.

And for Bibouf and Galibou, my enemies, I was even less! Nothing but a quadrumane, a baboon, an orangutan endowed with speech, not even a superior ape but an ape of lower status, since I did not climb trees!

Oh, it was necessary to get away! And for the remainder of the excursion, indifferent henceforth to the charms of the landscape and the delicacies of my friends, I no longer thought about anything but escape.

The captain yielded the helm to me for the return, and the boat traveled briskly, gliding under my hand without any hitch or difficulty.

How joyful the little centaurins were during that nautical excursion. They pranced and danced so much on the deck that they became inconvenient. They admired me, those children, amazed by the surety with which I launched the boat over he waves. They would have accompanied me out to sea with tranquility, without making any objection, all the way to Bordeaux!

No, my children, I won't abuse your confidence, I won't take you away from your charming island, your homeland. As for Bibouf and Galibou, that's another matter; we're at war!

I'm delighted! Everything is going well; I have the boat, the instrument of my escape. Let's prepare the continuation.

With Bibouf and Galibou, therefore, I undertook a few fishing trips at sea; sometimes we had the crew of the boat with us, sometimes the three of us went out alone. Amusing fishing trips, for the sea around the rocks was swarming with curious fish, strange beasts with vivid colors, bristling with horns and spikes on the head and he back, cleaving through the waves with long bizarre fins on every side.

I would certainly have been greatly amused if I had not had all the details of my flight to mull over. As for Bibouf and Galibou, they were sea-sick. So much the better; reduced to the state of parcels, they would give me less trouble.

So many things to prepare, so many difficulties to overcome. First of all, food supplies are necessary for a long crossing. By dint of calculation, of studying the stars and redrawing for the education of the little Kapalouias the map of the globe, I ended up determining the location of Centaur Island almost exactly.

It is far away, far away in the southern hemisphere, and...but no, allow me not to tell you either the longitude or the latitude. Later, when I've returned there, I'll make revelations; I'll tell all—but not before then, in order that no one cuts the grass from under my feet. It's necessary to be patient until then; I don't want any Amerigo Vespucci; I intended to remain the sole Christopher Columbus of Centaur Island. For the moment, know that it's a very long way away!

I had to count on three weeks of navigation, at least, in the most favorable circumstances, before perceiving land. Once there, I was saved. The French consulate, a telegram to Bordeaux announcing the extraordinary discovery to the stupefied world, embarkation on a large steamer with my boat and my two centaurs!

I need month's food supplies and a month's water for three of us. And God knows, centaurs have a demanding appetite! That's a major difficulty. I shall overcome it. Furthermore, as I can only count on myself for handling the boat, and I'll therefore have to confront enormous fatigues. I'll need to be in very good condition before departing. I must look after my health with particular care, and store up my strength. Let's do honor to friend Kapalouia's cuisine, then!

For food supplies, what can I do? I scarcely have the means to buy them, as my natural probity demands. I only have three sous in my pocket, and I don't believe they're current in the land. I had a hundred-franc banknote, but Kapalouia has taken possession of it and has put it in a place of honor in his drawing room.

Too bad—it will be necessary to be ingenious.

X. The eve of the great day!
A little musical soirée for
Madame Azuli Kapalouia's birthday

Nonchalantly sprawling in the garden of the Kapalouia villa, I am amusing myself watching the children play. They are running along the pathways, leaping over bushes like escaped colts and even trying to leap over the water jet of the fountain with a single bound without getting wet.

"Do the same, Zephyrin!" cries Karafalo.

"Little brat, you know full well that I don't have four feet and hocks of steel, like you."

I'm joyful; I have my good pipe in my mouth, with no tobacco inside, but the taste has remained, and gives me the illusion regardless. I'm joyful because everything is going well and I'm going shortly to make arrangements with Bibouf and Galibou for a sea trip—a real one, the Escape, finally!

Everything is arranged perfectly; only a few more details and we're there. It's set for tomorrow.

"Come on, Zephyrin, jump with me!"

"You've had enough jumping, little Topa. What about the French lesson, my friend? It's time; you're going to repeat to me right away the verb *être*...we're up to the imperfect of the subjunctive, the easiest bit. Shall we go?"

"Zephyrin, you're annoying me."

"I'll give you fifty lines! Come on, my subjunctive—you can gallop afterwards."

The little centaur raises his eyes to the havens, scratches is head, strikes he ground with his front hooves and commences in grumbling tone: "Imperfect of the subjunctive, was I being, were you being, were...were..."

"Well, well, children, are you going to be good and follow Zephyrin's lesson?" It's Kapalouia, who arrives and tries to calm the turbulence of the children.

"Yes, Papa! Yes, Papa!" cry the band. "He's the one who doesn't want to jump over the fountain!"

Little Mirako sets off at a run to embrace her father; she bumps into me and can't help knocking me over. I'm thrown to the ground by a seven-year-old child, that's a bit much! A little more and I'd bite the dust! At that age little centaurins are already weighty fellows. If I don't bring Bibouf and Galibou back to Europe, no one will want to believe me. But tomorrow will come.

"Look out, little madcap, you're going to hurt poor Zephyrin!" says Kapalouia. "Come on, my dear Zephyrin, make the decision to put on the artificial hind-quarters—that will give you stability, my friend, for, in truth, I can't understand how you maintain your equilibrium like that, on only two legs. I'd be heartbroken if little Mirako or one of her scatterbrained brothers broke your leg while playing."

So be it, I consent to everything. I don't want to cause that excellent friend pain at the moment of quitting him like this, surreptitiously, with all the appearances of ingratitude, for he has truly heaped me with benefits since my arrival. If I had fallen into the hands of the two scientists Bibouf and Galibou, who knows what would have become of me already? A collection item, a rare stuffed animal offered to the admiration of crowds in a Museum? I shiver at the thought!

A domestic brings the object, the wooden hindquarters of Mademoiselle Rakif's former toy. I think I look utterly ridiculous with it on...but after all, it's to please Kapalouia. The object is attached to my waist with a strong strap. Kapalouia gives me a centauran tunic in the latest fashion, which he drapes over the rump personally.

The children clap their hands.

"Very good, perfect," said Kapalouia, stepping back in order to see better. "Now you're like everyone else, a centaur of small size, it's true, but a centaur. Walk a little."

It's not very comfortable dragging that rump. It's made of light wood and here are little castors on the legs, but all the same, it doesn't go very well. I must make a funny sight with that, and they'd laugh uproariously in Bordeaux if they could see me. Kapalouia doesn't laugh, he thinks I look much better already with the artificial hindquarters. For him, I look less ridiculous than I did before.

"Would you like to take a little stroll with us like that?" asks Kapalouia. "We won't go very far, less than an hour from here?"

An hour, for Kapalouia, even going slowly, represents four or five leagues. I can't go five hundred meters with my artificial hindquarters. And I don't want to tire myself out—the great departure is set for tomorrow, I'm going to need all my vigor.

"No, my friend," I say, "I don't have the habit of it yet."

"Well, then, you can climb into the chariot; the domestic will pull you. We're bringing back flowers for my wife, today's her birthday. We won't be longer than two hours."

In order not to upset Kapalouia, and above all because of his wife's birthday, I consent to go on the excursion. I still have the afternoon to make my final preparations; that's sufficient.

The children have left already, frolicking. Kapalouia has my carriage hitched up—no, pardon me, he has he chariot brought out: a kind of handcart, long and deep, mounted on two low wheels, with long arms. I install myself in it; a centaur domestic picks up the handles and sets off at a trot. Kapalouia trots alongside me in order to chat; the children are capering ahead and behind, laughing and playing the fool.

I'll pass over the trip. Excellent. A fine garden, which I know already, furnishes us with bunches of flowers, which are put in the vehicle with me for the return journey. I disappear in the flowers and the foliage; I have the impression of receiving a triumph.

The triumph is set for tomorrow—or rather, the departure for the triumphant return to Europe.

In the afternoon I'll give Bibouf and Galibou their lesson. Everything is going very well. Bibouf and Galibou will talk about the planned trip of their own accord. We're going to fish a little further away, to the islets that can scarcely be distinguished on the horizon. We'll have to take lunch and dinner—a veritable picnic. They'll be laden down with food supplies; we'll take enough for two days, in case we have to camp on those rocks.

Bravo, very good, as much food as you wish; I warn you that at sea I always have a devouring appetite. That makes even more provisions, necessary for the great voyage.

I have to confess now one thing that has left me with remorse. I was getting ready to abuse the confidence of the benevolent Kapalouia and take advantage of the night to raid his larder, where I had seen a considerable provision of hams, large quantities of bananas, and other fruits. All that was, in sum, necessary

Yes, but what about probity? That tormented my conscience greatly. I ended up thinking about the hundred-franc bill that I had given Kapalouia.

I knew the prices of things; people live very cheaply on Centaur Island. Well, I would take exactly a hundred francs' worth! And then, later, when I had established communications between our old world and the island of the worthy centaurs, I would see Kapalouia again, I would give him my apologies for my slightly casual behavior, and he would quickly understand that I could not have one otherwise. What a pleasure I would have, in my turn, in receiving him in my estates, in my château…

That evening we had a little family celebration in the Kapalouia house. It was the anniversary of Madame Azuli's birth. It was very pleasant. The little ones recited very poetic compliments to their mother.

Secretly, I had taught one of La Fontaine's fables to Mademoiselle Mirako, and there as an explosion of bravos where the little centaurine, well-balanced on her legs, her eyes lowered, slightly emotional, commenced, in her rather amusing centauran accent: "Dear Maman, *The Ant and the Grasshopper*. The grasshopper, having been singing all summer, found itself very deprived…"

Then her big sister, Mademoiselle Rakif, whom her fiancé, the captain of the centaur archers, never quit with his eyes, took her piano on her knees—I'm mistaken, took a musical instrument of bizarre form, intermediate between a guitar and a piano, or at least bearing more resemblance to those instruments than to a hunting horn—and played a very brilliant piece, which made a great deal of noise, but which I shall not permit myself to judge, my musical knowledge not going much further than *Malbrough* or *My friend Pierrot*.

A charming soirée! The last one that I was to spend on Centaur Island—at least, I thought so! I was very cheerful. Believe me, in order to give an idea of our musical talents and to give my friends pleasure, I sang *Au clair de la lune*, and then the *Marseillaise*, and obtained as much success as Mademoiselle Rakif with her great piece.

The boat in which we were to set firth the following morning at seven o'clock was moored in the harbor, ten minutes from the Kapalouia house. Fortunately, there was no one aboard. The sailors were asleep in their houses, we were to leave without them. Bibouf and Galibou were confident.

When everyone was soundly asleep in the house I got up quietly and went to open the larder. Horror! I had to break in!

In sum, it was necessary. I made a dozen trips between the larder and the boat, and I heaped up fifteen large hams and an enormous supply of bananas in a huge crate under the deck.

I thought about the water, I filled two barrels from the limpid river that formed the little port and went to run into the sea half a league away.

Now, everything is ready! Tomorrow is the great day!

XI. The Escape.
To abduct or not to abduct?
Zephyrin makes the acquaintance of the fist of Pingo,
a centaur of the striped race

The great day dawned.

I put a short note of explanation and apologies on the drawing room table for my friend Kapalouia; I expressed—or, rather, tried to express in the centauran language—all my gratitude, and I announced to him that I would come back to see him as soon as I was able to organize an expedition…and I ran to the harbor while the family was still asleep.

At a quarter to seven I was on the boat and I was all ready to raise anchor as soon as Bibouf and Galibou were aboard.

Finally, here they come; I perceive them in the distance advancing gravely, followed by a striped centaur, their domestic, carrying an enormous basket of food under each arm. Very good.

Handshakes. I laugh as I look at them and they laugh too. For me, it's in thinking about the expressions on their faces when they find themselves in the open sea and begin to understand. O joy! I have them! I'm abducting my two enemies and taking them to Europe as pieces of evidence!

If I didn't have them with me, would anyone believe me in my homeland when I revealed my great discovery, the race of the centaurs of legend surviving far away, far away on the other side of the world, on a great island forming a sixth continent? No, I can see it from here; I'd be treated as a joker and people would laugh in my face!

But when people see them disembark, it will be necessary to yield to the evidence. What a surprise, what excitement in Bordeaux, in Paris, and in the Academies and Institutes of the entire world! What a triumph for me! Honors and a fortune, millions and medals, crowns and statues!

What will Bibouf and Galibou make of it all? I don't want to tell them anything before arriving in some port. Well, it's necessary to avoid a revolt on board. Even if they're laid out by sea-sickness, the two of them might inconvenience me. I have the intention, in any case, on the pretext of fearing bad weather and heavy seas, of locking them in the hold.

Have I to feel guilty about them? They're my personal enemies, they treat me as an improved chimpanzee and talk about having me stuffed for their Museum! My own intentions aren't as black...

I laugh internally and I can't help rubbing my hands. In spite of their habitual gravity, they manifest a certain gaiety.

"Everything is ready. Are you ready, Messieurs?"

"We're here, everything is perfectly in order," says Bibouf, rubbing the tip of his nose. "Everything is in order, isn't it, Galibou?"

"Admirably arranged," replied Galibou, departing from his habitual gravity with sniggers that make his spectacles jump up and down.

"Let's go, then! But what is your domestic waiting for before going ashore?"

"Our domestic? Pingo is coming with us. We're taking him—he might perhaps be useful to us in our little excursion. He knows how to sail; that might be of service if the occasion arises. Isn't that so, Pingo?"

"Yes," Pingo replies.

"But we have no need of him. I'm quite sufficient, as in our other fishing trips..."

"Bah! One never knows…it's a long way out to sea, where we're going..."

Oh yes, it's a long way, longer than you suspect, Bibouf, longer than you think, Galibou!

Argument. They absolutely insist on taking Pingo. That annoys me. I hesitate... I fear alarming them with a formal refusal. What if they were to renounce the excursion? Everything would be spoiled, all my plans overturned...

I reflect. After all, one passenger more is a complication, it increases the difficulty, even considerably… yes, but that further increases the triumph... Pingo is a centaur of the striped race, a race considered here as inferior, an enemy race that lives on the other side of the mountains, in regions less favored by nature, to which it has been driven back centuries ago after long and terrible wars. Here, that striped race primarily furnishes artisans of petty métiers, like sailing...

Well, what do the difficulties matter? It's an admirable opportunity that my two enemies are benevolently furnishing me, to bring back to Europe with them this specimen of the striped race. I examine Pingo from the corner of my eye; he looks very good, a superb specimen, vigorous and seemingly tough; his hindquarters display fine strips alternately black and white—a yellowish white and a bluish black. He'll have as much effect as the others in Bordeaux.

What luck that they have thought of Pingo! Let's go! Always provided that the worthy Pingo doesn't have sea-legs. I wish him a jolly sea-sickness in order that he doesn't inconvenience me too much.

The anchor is raised. A nice little breeze takes us gently down the river, and here comes the blue line of the ocean. A bar to cross and the boat will be skimming lightly over the first waves...

The weather is superb. The breeze fills my lungs and inflates our sails, the boat obeys the tiller meekly. Forward ho! Adieu—or rather, *au revoir*—charming island of good centaurs, magnificent land that I shall reveal to our old world! *Au revoir*, excellent Kapalouia, amiable family...don't think too badly of me, don't accuse me of ingratitude. I'll be back some day!

I set a course north-eastwards, by estimation, since I have no compass. I count on conserving that direction, with the permission of the wind, and reaching the great equatorial current, which, accelerating my speed, will carry me toward the western coast of South America.

After two hours of navigation, we've already covered a good distance. We can see a wide expanse of coast behind us. Centaur Island shows us a very jagged coast, a succession of points and capes, with large, deeply indented bays, beautiful extents of sand, rocky inlets in which verdure sometimes overflows to overhang the waves, and cliffs are sometimes superimposed on cliffs.

While steering I admire the landscape. I look forward in the direction of the old world, but from time to time my eyes turn back almost with regret toward the delightful island, the pleasant homeland of the good centaurs, which I'm fleeing thus...

The long chain of mountains stands out more clearly from here, fading away to the right and left into the blue, while in the center, in the background, above the blue-tinted ridges, white peaks loom up majestically, with long streaks of snow on their shoulders, floating over the entire island like an august assembly of patriarchs.

Perhaps I'm wrong to go; it's funny, I feel quite melancholy now.

It's Galibou who pulls me out of my reverie by scratching with his hoof behind me.

"Shall we have lunch?" he says.

I recover all the energy of my will. I revert to my plan. I'm on my way to triumph; let's not allow ourselves to be weakened by vain regrets.

"Let's have lunch," I say, joyfully.

Bibouf and Galibou don't seem to be suffering overmuch from sea-sickness today; they're only little pale. As for Pingo, the striped centaur, he doesn't appear to perceive in the slightest that he has quit the land...of centaurs.

We make a start on lunch: a game pâté, pancakes and tasty fruits, enormous grapes and bananas brought by those I'm already calling my victims. The sea-breeze gives one an appetite, and we honor the lunch fully. But be careful; a little moderation—let's not make too large a breach in our provisions!

Pingo, above all, exhibits an indiscreet appetite. He laughs, uncovering formidable teeth that worry me. That's because we have a long voyage in front of us and it's necessary not to empty the food-locker as soon as we leave. I can't say anything, but I wish them all a bout of sea-sickness to distract their appetite.

As I linger to dart one last glance in the direction of the island, Pingo takes hold of the tiller.

"Leave that, my friend," I say to him. "That's my affair."

"It's my turn," he replied. "I know, you'll see..."

And with a solid fist, he grabs my arm and moves me away.

Slightly anxious, I resign myself to letting him take the tiller. He does, in fact, know how to sail. Perhaps I shall have a few difficulties with this passenger. It's necessary that I find a way before this evening to make my three centaurs go down below the deck and lock them in. Not easy—but it's necessary!

Suddenly, I perceive that we're deviating from the route. We're bearing too far eastwards.

"Pingo, helm to port!" I say, with an authoritarian air.

Pingo doesn't seem to hear it. On the contrary, the boat veers more deliberately eastwards. We double a cape and a new coastline appears. It's the northern shore of the island. Instead of heading north-eastwards, the boat starts following the shore-line.

"Not that way," I say. "Pingo, give the tiller back to me."

"No!" says Bibouf, then.

"No!" says Galibou.

"That's not our route!"

"Yes. We've changed our plan, the fishing trip won't tell us anything more. You see, my friend Zephyrin, we've decided to show you the country. We're going that way, look, toward those great rockslides, can you see? That promontory is hiding the mouth of a river that comes from Zibor, our capital...a great city with fine monuments, academies, institutes and museums. Well, we're going to show you all that; you'll be delighted, it will interest you greatly."

"Come on, you're joking; we're only going for a little excursion."

"Kapalouia should have shown you all that a long time ago. And then again, you're expected; there's already been a great deal of talk about you out there—our report, you know…"

"Oh, let's talk about your report!" I shout, furiously. "I know about it, your report, my friend Kapalouia read it to me and explained it. Come on, no nonsense— let's resume our excursion, as was agreed."

I grasp of the tiller in order to take it from Pingo. He holds on to it solidly with his left hand and delivers a punch with the right that sends me sprawling against the side of the boat. He has the strength of a horse combined with the fist of a very muscular man, that animal of a striped zebra.

"Don't touch," he says to me, "or I thump you."

My plan is spoiled. I'm perplexed. What can I do? Alone against three burly fellows—for my old centaur scientists, after all, aren't as old as all that; they're solid individuals, and Pingo alone is worth as much as four boxers, four poor little men, for he has fists and also possesses four legs and four enormous iron-shod hooves. He might charge, and I can see that in a quarter of a minute he'd make mincemeat of four boxing champions! Let's not get annoyed, let's temporize, let's try to be clever, and shrewd. More cunning, always cunning!

XII. From calamity to calamity.
Bibouf and Galibou reveal themselves.
How the quadrumane Zephyrin disembarked
in the centaur capital incognito

My plan is going badly. We have been following the northern coast of the island for a long time; it's four o'clock in the afternoon and we've reached the mouth of the great river that comes from the capital.

I'm no longer saying anything. Let's face up to fortune bravely. It's only a postponement, and I'll succeed in abducting my three centaurs another time, perhaps when we return from our excursion.

"Do you see that port at the mouth of the river?" Bibouf says to me. "We're heading straight for it, but we're not stopping, we're going directly to Zibor, three or four hours upriver..."

"What will our friend Kapalouia think when he doesn't see us return?"

"He can think what he likes. In any case, he'll receive a letter in which I inform him that we've borrowed you in the interests of science. I explain to him that you're a great curiosity of natural history and that he's acting badly in keeping you, so to speak, under wraps in his home, uniquely for his own personal satisfaction, without taking account of the rights of science."

"And what if I don't want to go with you?"

"Yes, yes, you want to! You're going to see the country, its advantageous for your education. And I assure you that everywhere we go, you'll be received with consideration by scientists as well as simple curiosity-seekers. We've prepared the way; you're expected, my little friend. You interest everyone; be proud—you're going to have your picture in the newspapers!"

Damn, I thought, *what a setback! Such a well-planned escape! These fellow have caused me to lose all the fruit of all my pains. When will I find another opportunity? I'll wait, so be it, I'll wait! Let's be cunning. I need my revenge!*

After a pause of a few minutes in the port, we set forth on the river, three or four hundred meters wide at its mouth, which descended through a beautiful wooded valley, in which every turning showed us pretty groups of habitations on the slopes of the hills and in tranquil inlets sheltered under the verdure of great trees.

We traversed fine cultivated fields, gilded all the way to the horizon by the undulations of rope crops; I'm not very well up on agriculture, but I'm sure that there were cereals there as we have here, species not very distant from ours.

Pingo had lowered the sail as soon as we entered the river. He had thrown a rope to the bank and two vigorous centaurs were hauling our boat, trotting side by side along a towpath From time to time we passed other boats laden with wood or bales, being hauled downriver in the same fashion.

There are no factory chimneys on the route. The centaurs have no large industry; they only have the good old eternal crafts, the simple and healthy family industries. Agriculture, above all, is in honor, the excellent soil furnishes the necessary products without avarice. Everywhere along the river, as in Kapalouia's homeland, there are only agrarian regions, idyllic landscapes animated by a few silhouettes of centaurs galloping through the fields, or families of laborers at work, scattered through the meadows. I've told you that life was simple and mild, and the mores patriarchal...

I admired it, but while cursing internally, darting furious glances at my two crooks and that brute Pingo.

At about eight o'clock in the evening, as night was falling, Bibouf showed me in the distance an agglomeration of houses gilded by the setting sun. We were passing gardens and beautiful villas, reflected in the river, which announced to us the proximity of a large city. It was Zibor, the capital.

"We're arriving, my little friend," Bibouf told me. "Zibor is a great city, with sixty thousand inhabitants. We want to spare you, and us too, the annoyances of public curiosity as we disembark. You can imagine that idlers would flock to see you, little singular and original creature. What a crowd! No, no premature exhibition; we intend to reserve the first fruits for the Academies..."

"What?" I said, pricking up my ears.

"Yes, we'll disembark incognito. Pingo, go fetch the crate.

Pingo went down below decks and reappeared, pulling a large crate with his muscular arms, which I recognized immediately. It was the one inside which I had heaped up all my provisions for the great voyage.

Pingo seemed surprised as he deposited it on the deck. Bibouf immediately removed the lid.

"What all this?"

Pingo scattered my fifteen hams, my pancakes and bananas—all the provisions I had accumulated—on the deck. Bibouf and Galibou looked at them, astonished.

"When Pingo brought the crate on board yesterday evening, it was empty," said Galibou. "What does this signify?"

I thought it prudent to appear as surprised as them, and I tasted a banana, with an innocent expression. Bibouf and Galibou shook their heads. Evidently, they suspected something. Fatality!

"My little friend," said Galibou, in a dry tone, "We're going to send all this back to Kapalouia. Let's not mention it again! Except that this demonstrates that we need to be prudent and vigilant. Now, let's think about preserving your incognito…into the crate!"

"What?" I said, recoiling.

"Get into it, cunning little animal! We're going to a hostelry where our arrival has been announced. Get in— it's in order that no one will see you on the way."

I stood before my two enemies and I looked them under the chin with a defiant expression.

"Monsieur Galibou, Monsieur Bibouf," I cried, "You're beginning to annoy me. I won't get into that crate; my dignity opposes it."

I didn't think about Pingo. His fist fell upon me from behind; he seized me by the collar and by the belt, and before I could say *oof*, I was in the crate. The lid closed on me, and on my dignity, forced to make its decision.

The rogues! They had me, I was completely in their power. What were they going to do with me?

I heard Pingo fasten the lid with a strong catch that I had noticed. I shivered. I would choke, rapidly asphyxiated, in that narrow crate, which reeked horribly of ham. I started hammering the sides with mighty kicks, but they were very solid, alas.

On one of its sides, however, Pingo slid a few grooved panels. Everything had been foreseen; the crate was fitted out in such a fashion that air and light could enter. I was no longer running the risk of choking, and I found myself in a sort of cage.

"Don't worry, my little friend," Galibou said to me. "You're wrong to be annoyed, we intend to treat you gently. We've arrived, we're going to disembark. Be good, or we'll be obliged to close the crate again.

What was the point of struggling? My impotence in their hands was complete. I exhorted myself to be patient. Let's see what happens; a means of escaping my kidnappers will end up presenting itself.

We disembarked. The boat was moored to a shadowed quay, in the midst of other boats of various sizes. The river was no longer more than a hundred meters wide. Alongside us I had time to see a ferry, very broad and very long, maneuvered by two centaurs naked to the waist. Further away, a humpbacked bridge with five arches, very high in the middle arch, as in the Oriental lands, straddled the river. Bibouf told me that it connected the two finest quarters of the city.

A cart advanced pulled by a centaur porter. Pingo and the ported lifted up my cage carefully and loaded me on to the cart with Bibouf's and Galibou's luggage, and we departed at a gentle trot.

*XIII. Captain Zephyrin, a natural curiosity of the first
order, has the honors of a very flattering poster*

A new existence was commencing for me, alas. Until then, everything had been too pleasant. I was free, happy ad pampered in Kapalouia's house; that excellent creature showed himself full of concern and heaped me with marks of amity. His charming children liked me too; they could not get enough of their biped friend; in sum, I was almost a member of the family.

Whereas now, O calamity, in the power of Bibouf, Galibou and Pingo, I was no longer anything but a curious animal, often locked in a cage, always closely watched, dragged from town to town...and exhibited, to complete the humiliation, exhibited for money!

Where are you, Kapalouia, my friend? All this, alas, is doubtless the punishment for my black ingratitude toward you; I wanted to flee from you, and I've fallen into the hands of Bibouf and Galibou, the very individuals that I wanted to take to Bordeaux in order to introduce them to the scientific world!

But I'll resume the story of my misfortunes.

In the house to which the cart transported me Pingo had my crate transported to a large room where there was a bed for him. W supped together in that room, me sitting in the Turkish fashion in my crate, the others facing me on a high table.

I have to admit that I was treated well. Bibouf and Galibou even affected to be gracious in order to soothe me. They announced to me that I was going to lead a charming life, to be introduced into high centauran society, introduced to scientists, to the luminaries of Literature and the Arts, all interested already by what had been said about me in the newspapers and impatient to study me. They said that the king would doubtless come to see me and that I would have the honor of being taken to the palace before the royal family.

They added that, in my petty intellect, I ought to take account of all the pleasure and the immense advantages of that new existence: I would be famous, it was almost glory; I would see the country and meet illustrious centaurs; people of all classes would file before me...and I ought to testify some gratitude to them, Bibouf and Galibou, who had assumed the responsibility, at their own expense, of procuring me that delightful existence, those honors, those pleasures and those mental distractions!

Personally, I'm made in such a way that emotions and worries put me to sleep. I gain from that by more easily recovering strength and courage. I had had more than sufficient emotions that day, so I fell asleep on the cushions that Pingo passed me in my cage before the end of my enemies' speech.

Serious matters, tomorrow!

The next day, when I woke up, Pingo opened my cage and said to me, speaking pidgin: "You know, little animal, you free, you not attached by cord, provided you not try to run away...anyway, you watched, me not leave you. Look, me like you a lot already. Me going to give you pleasure."

Why not respond to those advances? Certainly, I wanted Pingo to go to the devil, but why tell him that? Let's try, on the contrary, to gain his sympathy.

"Me your friend too, Pingo. You good fellow, Pingo. Me like you a lot."

O hypocrisy! I emphasized that declaration of amity by shaking my jailer's hand.

"Here," Pingo goes on. "You can read a little. Look what's to be posted at the door of the house—it's for you, my friend, you well content."

He showed me, leaning against the wall, a large placard bearing a long inscription in characters of various sizes. Slowly, I spell out:

Next week
The quadrumane Zephyrin
after which he will be presented to illustrious scientists
of various ACADEMIES
gathered in special congress in honor
of this presentation
by the learned masters of zoology and paleontology
BIBOUF & GALIBOU,
the extraordinary creature, the singular talking and
thinking quadrumane
Zephyrin
??? Vestige of unknown world or strange phenomenon,
bizarre being
escaped from the strata of the Tertiary epoch, having
survived, who knows how,
the revolutions of the globe ???
Will be visible for the Public here for a month
at the price of two silver piecettes per person,
one piecette for children,
gratis for military personnel.
Tell your friends
Director of the exhibition: Pingo

I understood everything now! O rage! Bibouf and Galibou had had the same idea as me and the wretched had got in ahead of me. Fatality! If I had put more haste into my preparations it would have been me who abducted them, it would have been me who was drafting posters of the same sort in Bordeaux or in Paris. But let's not try to rebel, let's think instead!

I didn't get any further in my reflections; breakfast arrived, Bibouf and Galibou came in.

"Well, have you read the poster?" Galibou asked me.

"I've read it, "I replied. "I'm most honored… it's very flattering. It's too much honor for me…"

"No, no, don't be modest, you're a curiosity of the first order. And you'll impassion the public, you'll see! You'll excite discussions and controversies…yes, scientific quarrels…it's starting already!"

"We've opened fire," said Bibouf, rubbing his hands. "Personally, I proclaim that you're barely emerged from the lowest animality, that you're a simple brute with glimmers of reason, while my learned colleague Galibou sustains the contrary thesis…a matter of triggering polemics, in your interest, since it's in the interest of the enterprise. My eminent colleague Galibou, modifying his opinion since our first communication to the Academies, claims that you're the representative of a decadent species, isn't that right, learned Galibou?"

"Certainly," Galibou agreed.

"…Of a species that's extinct, that finished because of an excess of intellectuality. Do you understand these things? Look at your muscles by comparison with Pingo's… you scarcely seem equipped for fighting…"

I bowed by head humbly, determined not to argue with them and to give them the idea that I was absolutely resigned to my fate.

"Let's have breakfast," Galibou went on. "We're expected this morning at the Zoological Institute, and this afternoon at the session of the Academies. Tomorrow, a presentation at the Fine Arts, a session of portraits and measurements. For the afternoon, I've solicited an audience at the Palace, it's necessary to appear before the King and Her Majesty the Queen. What honors! What honors!"

"Yes," I said, "but what will my friend Kapalouia think of you, on not seeing us come back?"

"Kapalouia? He's informed," said Bibouf. "He knows that in taking you away, we were only yielding to your insistence..."

"What, you said that?"

"Certainly, and furthermore, you wrote it to him yourself."

"Me?"

"Yes. Do you recall that I asked you for an autograph the other day? The autograph was the signature for a letter that I wrote afterwards...in your name, with the necessary spelling mistakes."

Infernal Bibouf! He had thought of everything! I too had left a letter for Kapalouia on leaving, but it was necessarily conceived in vague terms, by reason of my feeble knowledge of the centauran language. Kapalouia wouldn't understand, and would think that I had left with Bibouf of my own free will!

I've been presented to the Institute of Zoology, presented at liberty, as they say in circuses and menageries. I was taken through the streets in my crate covered with drapes. Bibouf and Galibou don't like waste; it's necessary that the passers-by don't see me without shelling out the fee of two silver piecettes.

The Institute of Zoology occupies one wing of a vast edifice in which there are amphitheaters for lectures and galleries for collections, exactly like those here.

On arrival, Pingo opened my cage and, preceded by Bibouf and Galibou, I was taken into a beautiful hall were a large number of centaurs were gathered mostly bald old messieurs in spectacles, who uttered exclamations on seeing me.

I was immediately surrounded, examined, turned this way and that. Bibouf made a little introductory speech. Galibou spoke in his turn, and then there was a hubbub of animated discussions and loud arguments, almost disputes, for two full hours, of which I didn't understand very much, except that all those eminent zoologists were far from being in agreement as to my true nature. Some talked about trickery and were absolutely convinced that I was an amputated centaur to whom an ape's legs had been adapted, unless I was a pure phenomenon, a monstrous error of nature. Bibouf and Galibou had to argue for a long time to pulverize the skepticism of some of their savant colleagues—but how they rubbed their hands on the return journey!

The afternoon was occupied in the same fashion. I appeared before other scientists, physicians and philosophers, who studied me for three hours, made me talk, walk, jump and run, taking copious notes, and after the end of a stormy session they went away in groups, which continued a lively and animated discussion all along the street, where surprised centaur shopkeepers watched them gesticulating.

"It's going well," said Galibou. "The polemics are about to commence."

The next day, taken o the Temple of the Arts, I had the opportunity to perceive centaur painting and sculpture. I'm not a connoisseur, and I probably wouldn't be able to tell the difference between a Leonardo da Vinci and a contemporary impressionist if it weren't for the cracks indicating the age of the Leonardo, but I can say that the centaurs don't seem to be to be very well endowed with regard to the Fine Arts.

That doubtless comes from their impetuous nature, which tends to active occupations rather than meticulous endeavors. Certainly, if Raphael and Michelangelo had had four muscular legs as indefatigable as theirs, they wouldn't have produced as many masterpieces, and of lesser quality; without a doubt, Raphael and Michelangelo would have preferred galloping joyously through the meadows and the woods, the plains and the mountains.

My self-esteem had to suffer somewhat among the centaur artists, I saw a great many disdainful expressions and I overheard a few uncomplimentary remarks.

"The height of the body, all right, although the chest, shoulders and arms of the quadrumane are feeble, but the rest is quite disgraceful!"

"What a lack of harmony and proportion in the ensemble!"

236

"What weakness in those two miserable little legs, which transport him with difficulty at a slow pace!"

etc...

Firmly determined not to take offense at anything, I contented myself with enclosing myself in my dignity, while I was sketched standing up, sitting down or walking.

The following day was the solemn day of the royal audience. The large Centaur Island has enjoyed a rather advanced civilization for centuries; it has seen the petty principalities that once divided it disappear; the fusion of the various tribes has taken place over time, and nothing any longer remains but a single immense federated kingdom, with viceroys descended from ancient chiefs in the provinces. The southern part of the island, inhabited by the centaurs of the more primitive and less civilized striped race, is a sort of colony of that kingdom, or if you like, a tributary province, conquered in the past by long wars.

I was therefore admitted to appear before His Majesty, a centaur in the prime of life, of proud and haughty bearing, representing a dynasty that already counted twenty-three kings, among whom, it was said, there were a number of remarkable monarchs. I saw the Queen, a mild and likeable centauress of about thirty, who gave me her royal hand to kiss with a charming grace.

The young princes reminded me of the children of my friend Kapalouia by their vivacity and mischievousness.

His Majesty charged Bibouf with having my full-length portrait painted for his cabinet of curiosities. He congratulated Bibouf and Galibou and accorded them decorations. As for me, who earned them those decorations and, in consequence, deserved them more than they did. His Majesty only gave me a pair of bracelets of a metal resembling silvered copper.

Oh, when I get Bibouf, Galibou and Pingo to Bordeaux!

The end of the week resembled the beginning; I made the acquaintance of all the notable individuals in the capital. It was always the same; at first sight I excited a keen astonishment that was quite flattering, but afterwards, in the speeches and conversations, I caught a number of criticisms that were more or less disagreeable to hear.

All those rather tiring official presentations had the advantage of introducing me to a host of interesting individuals and furnishing with notions of the institutions of Centaur Island precious for the relation of my voyage, my misfortunes and my captivity to be written on my return to my homeland, so I didn't neglect to take notes.

Now, O humiliation, we arrive at the public exhibition.

One morning, Pingo said to me: "Come along then, your new apartment is ready, you'll be content!"

I had heard centaur carpenters or metalworkers hammering, filing, and driving in nails without thinking that it was for my benefit. Pingo took me through a courtyard and into the gardens. At the back, under a hangar closed by sliding doors, I perceived a large square cage about five meters by four, provided with solid iron bars and fitted at the top with rolling blinds, to close all four sides completely in case of need.

Bibouf and Galibou were there, making a last inspection.

"You see, my dear Zephyrin," Galibou said to me, "extremely precious little animal, last representative of a race of mammals disappeared from the entire surface of

238

the globe, that you'll be very comfortable in this new apartment."

"My dear Galibou," I said, sharply, "I've noticed that, although a centaur, you possess a few vague sentiments of humanity; I appeal to those sentiments! You're not going to lock me in there!"

"But yes, it's necessary! You'll be very comfortable, it's nice here, in the fresh air of the garden, under the lovely shade..."

"Me, in captivity! In a cage, as in the Jardin des Plantes! Me, Zephyrin Canigousse, long-haul captain!"

"You dare to complain, precious little animal, but we could have made a gift of you to the Museum, and who knows whether, in order better to preserve you in your present state, you wouldn't have been immediately naturalized and placed under glass, sheltered from any accident? Instead of that, Bibouf and I are making sacrifices, offering you an existence full of amusements and distractions..."

"And you're still complaining!" groaned Bibouf. "You're still protesting!"

"Distractions you shall have in abundance," Galibou went on. "The public will come, people of all classes, there'll be comings and goings. People will talk to you, you'll have conversation, people will say amiable things to you. You'll only be in that cage for your receptions, during the day, from ten o'clock until five; the rest of the time you'll come up to our apartment, or we'll go out together, we'll go for a stroll, you'll take exercise..."

"You won't try to run away," Bibouf went on. "It's not in your interest, my friend. First of all, where would you go? With your ridiculous conformation, you can't go very quickly. Then, you'd be recognized and brought back here without delay...unless dishonest men stole

239

you, but for that we have law courts. That's not all, one day a week the price of entry changes; it's no longer two piecettes that people pay to see you, it's ten. Ten, my little friend, that's flattering for you! That day, naturally, you'll only have a select public, you'll take tea with people of the highest society..."

"See how delicate we are," added Galibou. "Pingo wanted to plant a tree in your cage, and people would have demanded that you climb it in order to do a few exercises, as you must do in your homeland, but we've divined that that would annoy you and we've got rid of the tree. You can therefore do as you wish in the cage; we'll give you books, games, pencils, you can write, you can devote yourself to works of some sort to demonstrate that you have a certain intelligence. As I said to Pingo, that way you'll become a much more interesting little phenomenon. But Pingo is at the cash register, and he's already signaling to me that the public is here already, and it's only half past nine. It's a success, my friend, a success!"

*XV. Return of the quadrumane Zephyrin to his homeland
after seventeen years and three months of captivity*

Yes, it was a success. From the morning onwards a numerous public crowded into the garden in front of my cage, centaurs of all social classes, workers, peasants on market days, bourgeois centaurs with their families, a great many children, and even, sometimes, schoolchildren brought by their masters and mistresses—at discount prices.

Pingo was the titular director of the exhibition, the "Manager," as the English say. Bibouf and Galibou remained in the wings, outside vile questions of money; they were content to supervise and organize. From time to time, one or other of them gave a scientific lecture.

I was well treated. From day to day, the two scoundrels became increasingly amiable. That was because they were raking in superb receipts, sometimes as many as seven or eight hundred piecettes, and five times that on distinguished days. I represented a considerable capital, so they heaped me with consideration and strove to find distractions for me.

We took hygienic strolls every evening. Pingo put me in the crate to traverse the city, but as soon as we were in the country. I got out and walked, philosophizing with the two scientists, under the surveillance of the vigilant Pingo.

Let's be cunning, let's be patient, let's wait, I said to myself. *The opportunity will eventually come to give my captors the slip and return to my homeland...or rather, no, I won't give them the slip; no, I'll escape, but I want to take them with me in my flight, to abduct all three of them…O vengeance! My old plan still remains good, it's just a matter of being patient, of finding a way, of being ingenious, in order to engender the opportunity…*

And I waited! And do you know how long I was on the lookout for that opportunity, how long I remained captive, behind my bars, in the power of my persecutors?

Seventeen years!

I lived for seventeen years on Centaur Island, seventeen years and three or four months, without succeeding in finding the saving stratagem, the possible plan for getting away from Pingo and returning home, where, although a bachelor, I nevertheless had relatives and friends who must be anxious about the length of my absence! I didn't stay in the centaur capital for more than eighteen months, during which Bibouf and Galibou used the most ingenious means to maintain the curiosity of the inhabitants: debates, polemics and even little lectures given my me, for I quickly arrived at being able to speak the centauran language fluently—lectures on humankind, its mores, its customs, its nations, etc.

Afterwards, we left for long tours of the provinces. In the utmost depths of the island, there was no point of thinking of escape. I was patient, for we had to end up eventually in the coastal provinces. But in the coastal cities, Bibouf and Galibou were suspicious, I sensed their narrower surveillance. Pingo never quit me. I talked about bathing, excursions on the sea during the summer—which lasted for three quarters of the year—but it fell on deaf ears; the odious Pingo sniggered…

Alas, I ended up renouncing my original plan, nurtured for so long, and the hope of taking them with me in order to take them to Europe. I was no longer thinking of any but one thing, of fleeing, all alone, but of fleeing!

I escaped more than once; I wandered on the shore, seeking in vain to take possession of some kind of boat, but I had to go back, thwarted, every time, to wait for a better opportunity.

Yes, that existence lasted seventeen years! Bibouf and Galibou, heaped with honors, having become illustrious scientists, thanks to me, members of all the institutes on the island, ended up yielding me completely to Pingo, only reserving full property in my body following my death, for, as a supreme honor, my skull was demanded by the Academy of Sciences, and my place in the Museum was already prepared.

With Pingo my appearances took on a less scientific character. That centaur had the mentality of an exhibitor of bears. I had to deliver myself to a few exercises in public, to sing, to dance, to perform acrobatics and deploy a few petty talents. Yes, we had become fairground performers!

I saw the country with him. For some time we traveled in the regions of the striped centaurs. Briefly, I thought about fomenting revolt among them and seeking to provoke them to rise up against their powerful neighbors. I conspired…and then I felt remorse. That island of centaurs was living happily and peacefully in the sunlight of the Pacific Ocean. Was I going to trouble that happiness? No, let's think of something else!

Finally, Pingo launched me in the theater. The centaurs only have open air theaters, always placed in marvelous locations, where plays are performed of the genre of our tragedies, with choruses, as among the Greeks, and sometimes also dramas of a more modern taste.

A fashionable author wrote a play expressly for me in which I played a brief but important role. I saw my name in large letters on the posters: *The Quadrumane Zephyrin*.

In that play I was, it's necessary to confess, a sort of ape, an orangutan or a gorilla, and I stole the child of a rich family of centaurs in order to carry him away to my natal forest.

That was what the author in question made of me! No matter, he was the one who furnished me with the means of my escape. May he accept all my thanks!

In the provinces, we gave a series of performances of *The Perfidious Quadrumane*. I linked myself in amity with two centaur artistes, my fellow actors in the play, in which they played the father and the mother of the stolen centaurin. Those worthy folk, without prejudices in my regard, treated me as a comrade. We often chatted about my homeland, about Bordeaux, Paris and Europe, whose inhabitants were by no means quadrumane savages, as the scientists of Centaur Island claimed...

And I proposed to them that they depart with me for that unknown and marvelous world. I made hopes of fortune shine in their eyes, assuring them, by legal contract, of an honest partnership.

In the end, they gave in. We were on the coast at the time, not far from the place where I had once been cast ashore. With their savings and mine—for I received a modest wage that provided me with pocket money—they secretly bought a boat, and then food supplies for six weeks. One day, after the performance, I forced one of the bars in my cage-bedroom, reached the beach where they were waiting for me, and we leapt aboard our boat.

With what celerity I hosted the sail, with what an explosion of joy I seized the tiller and headed out to sea. It was just in time, moreover. Pingo arrived, galloping along the shore anxiously. He mistook us for fishers and hailed us to ask us whether we had seen a kind of chimpanzee with the face of a centaur, mounted on two paltry legs, wandering around.

Saved! Finally! And I was about to being back to my homeland two specimens of the centauran race! Triumph in the end, after so many years!

In order to reach the open sea we had to travel for some distance along the shore through a line of islets and reefs. It was necessary to be prudent and not run aground on departure. Fortunately, the moon was shining brightly and the boat steered well. Between all those rocks however, the waves became a trifle rough, and we began to dance. Then the enthusiasm of my two friends waned rapidly, sea-sickness caused their fine resolutions to capsize. After having struggled for three-quarters of an hour, they collapsed piteously on the deck, and renounced everything: the fine voyage, the glory, the fortune. They even threatened…

What could I do? I reasoned, I argued, I begged. I refused categorically to return to land and tried to make them go below decks in order to lock them in. When they saw that I was determined not to yield, they recovered a little energy. They got up, unsteadily, and leapt into the sea. The coast was not far away; I saw them swimming vigorously and, after a good quarter of an hour, go ashore in an inlet.

Adieu, dreams of fortune, lets save ourselves first! And alone, in my feeble boat, I set sail for the high seas.

After six weeks of navigation, horribly fatiguing, a week of tempests when I nearly perished a hundred times over, my boat is falling apart. Fortunately the great equatorial current carries me without too much difficulty. Finally, land appears, our land, the world of human beings! It's the coast of South America...ships in sight...men...a port...

It's Valparaiso... Saved! I'm saved!

There I find a ship for Bordeaux, which repatriates me, and I reach home after an absence of eighteen years.

That's my great adventure. I haven't said anything; no one would have believed me, since I didn't bring back anything to show. If I'm talking about it now, it's because, having recovered from my fatigues, having taken the time to ripen my plans and organize my expedition in silence, I'm preparing to set forth again any day now, well equipped and well accompanied, for Centaur Island, in order to rediscover it and give the world its sixth continent.

And this time, by no matter what means, I intend absolutely to bring back Pingo, Bibouf and Galibou!

SF & FANTASY

Adolphe Alhaiza. *Cybele*
Alphonse Allais. *The Adventures of Captain Cap*
Henri Allorge. *The Great Cataclysm*
Guy d'Armen. *Doc Ardan: The City of Gold and Lepers; The Troglodytes of Mount Everest/The Giants of Black Lake; The Abominable Snowman*
G.-J. Arnaud. *The Ice Company*
André Arnyvelde. *The Ark; The Mutilated Bacchus*
Charles Asselineau. *The Double Life*
Henri Austruy. *The Eupantophone; The Olotelepan; The Petitpaon Era*
Barillet-Lagargousse. *The Final War*
Barbot de Villeneuve.*The Naiads/Beauty & The Beast*
Cyprien Bérard. *The Vampire Lord Ruthwen*
S. Henry Berthoud. *Martyrs of Science; The Angel Asrael*
Aloysius Bertrand. *Gaspard de la Nuit*
Richard Bessière. *The Gardens of the Apocalypse; The Masters of Silence*
Chevalier de Béthune. *The World of Mercury*
Albert Bleunard. *Ever Smaller*
Félix Bodin. *The Novel of the Future*
Pierre Boitard. *Journey to the Sun*
Louis Boussenard. *Monsieur Synthesis*
Alphonse Brown. *City of Glass; The Conquest of the Air*
Émile Calvet. *In a Thousand Years*
André Caroff. *The Terror of Madame Atomos; Miss Atomos; The Return of Madame Atomos; The Mistake of Madame Atomos; The Monsters of Madame Atomos; The Revenge of Madame Atomos; The Resurrection of Madame Atomos; The Mark of Madame Atomos; The Spheres of Madame Atomos; The Wrath of Madame Atomos* (w/M. & Sylvie Stéphan); *The Sins of Madame Atomos* (w/M. & Sylvie Stéphan)
Jean Carrère. *The End of Atlantis*
Félicien Champsaur. *Homo-Deus; The Human Arrow; Nora, The Ape-Woman; Ouha, King of the Apes; Pharaoh's Wife*
Didier de Chousy. *Ignis*
Jules Clarétie. *Obsession*
Jacques Collin de Plancy. *Voyage to the Center of the Earth*
Michel Corday. *The Eternal Flame; The Lynx* (w/André Couvreur)

André Couvreur. *Caresco, Superman; The Exploits of Professor Tornada* (3 vols.); *The Necessary Evil*
Gaston Danville. *The Perfume of Lust*
Camille Debans. *The Misfortunes of John Bull*
Captain Danrit. *Undersea Odyssey*
C. I. Defontenay. *Star (Psi Cassiopeia)*
Charles Derennes. *The People of the Pole*
Georges Dodds (anthologist). *The Missing Link*
Charles Dodeman. *The Silent Bomb*
Harry Dickson. *The Heir of Dracula; Harry Dickson vs. The Spider*
Jules Dornay. *Lord Ruthven Begins*
Alfred Driou. *The Adventures of a Parisian Aeronaut*
Odette Dulac. *The War of the Sexes*
Alexandre Dumas. *The Return of Lord Ruthven; The Man who Married a Mermaid* (w/P. Lacroix)
Renée Dunan. *Baal; The Ultimate Pleasure*
J.-C. Dunyach. *The Night Orchid; The Thieves of Silence*
Henri Duvernois. *The Man Who Found Himself*
Achille Eyraud. *Voyage to Venus*
Henri Falk. *The Age of Lead*
Paul Féval. *Anne of the Isles; Knightshade; Revenants; Vampire City; The Vampire Countess; The Wandering Jew's Daughter*
Paul Féval, *fils. Felifax, the Tiger-Man*
Charles de Fieux. *Lamékis*
Fernand Fleuret. *Jim Click*
Charles-Marie Flor O'Squarr. *Phantoms*
Louis Forest. *Someone is Stealing Children in Paris*
Arnould Galopin. *Doctor Omega; Doctor Omega and the Shadowmen* (anthology)
Judith Gautier. *Isoline and the Serpent-Flower*
H. Gayar. *The Marvelous Adventures of Serge Myrandhal on Mars*
Louis Geoffroy. *The Apocryphal Napoleon*
G.L. Gick. *Harry Dickson and the Werewolf of Rutherford Grange*
Raoul Gineste. *The Second Life of Doctor Albin*
Delphine de Girardin. *Balzac's Cane*
Emmanuel Gorlier. *The Nyctalope and the Tower of Babel*
Léon Gozlan. *The Vampire of the Val-de-Grâce*
Jules Gros. *The Fossil Man*
Jimmy Guieu. *The Polarian-Denebian War* (2 vols.)
Edmond Haraucourt. *Daah, the First Human; Illusions of Immortality*
Nathalie Henneberg. *The Green Gods*

Eugène Hennebert. *The Enchanted City*

Jules Hoche. *The Maker of Men and His Formula*

V. Hugo, P. Foucher & P. Meurice. *The Hunchback of Notre-Dame*

Romain d'Huissier. *Hexagon: Dark Matter*

Jules Janin. *The Magnetized Corpse*

Gustave Kahn. *The Tale of Gold and Silence*

Gérard Klein. *The Mote in Time's Eye; Starmasters*

Fernand Kolney. *Love in 5000 Years*

Paul Lacroix. *Danse Macabre; The Man who Married a Mermaid* (w/Alexandre Dumas)

Louis-Guillaume de La Follie. *The Unpretentious Philosopher*

Jean de La Hire. *The Fiery Wheel; Enter the Nyctalope; The Nyctalope on Mars; The Nyctalope vs. Lucifer; The Nyctalope Steps In; Night of the Nyctalope; Return of the Nyctalope; The Nyctalope and the Tower of Babel*

Etienne-Léon de Lamothe-Langon. *The Virgin Vampire*

André Laurie. *Spiridon*

Gabriel de Lautrec. *The Vengeance of the Oval Portrait*

Alain le Drimeur. *The Future City*

Georges Le Faure & Henri de Graffigny. *The Extraordinary Adventures of a Russian Scientist Across the Solar System* (2 vols.)

Gustave Le Rouge. *The Dominion of the World* (w/G. Guitton) (4 vols.); *The Mysterious Doctor Cornelius* (3 vols.); *The Vampires of Mars*

Jules Lermina. *The Battle of Strasbourg; Mysteryville; Panic in Paris; The Secret of Zippelius; To-Ho and the Gold Destroyers*

Maurice Level. *The Gates of Hell*

André Lichtenberger. *The Centaurs; The Children of the Crab*

Maurice Limat. *Mephista*

Listonai. *The Philosophical Voyager*

Jean-Marc & Randy Lofficier. *Edgar Allan Poe on Mars; The Katrina Protocol; Pacifica 1, 2; Robonocchio; Return of the Nyctalope;* (anthologists) *Tales of the Shadowmen 1-14; The Vampire Almanac* (2 vols.)

Ch. Lomon & P.-B. Gheuzi. *The Last Days of Atlantis*

Charles Malato. *Lost!*

Maurice Magre. *The Marvelous Story of Claire d'Amour; The Call of the Beast; Priscilla of Alexandria; The Angel of Lust; The Mystery of the Tiger; The Poison of Goa; Lucifer; The Blood of Toulouse; The Albigensian Treasure; Jean de Fodoas; Melusine; The Brothers of the Virgin Gold*

Victor Margueritte. *The Bacheloress; The Companion; The Couple*
Camille Mauclair. *The Virgin Orient*
Xavier Mauméjean. *The League of Heroes*
Joseph Méry. *The Tower of Destiny*
Hippolyte Mettais. *Paris Before the Deluge; The Year 5865*
Louise Michel. *The Human Microbes; The New World*
Tony Moilin. *Paris in the Year 2000*
Michael Moorcock's *Legends of the Multiverse*
José Moselli. *Illa's End*
John-Antoine Nau. *Enemy Force*
Marie Nizet. *Captain Vampire*
Charles Nodier. *Trilby and The Crumb Fairy*
C. Nodier, A. Beraud & Toussaint-Merle. *Frankenstein*
Henri de Parville. *An Inhabitant of the Planet Mars*
Gaston de Pawlowski. *Journey to the Land of the 4th Dimension*
Georges Pellerin. *The World in 2000 Years*
Ernest Pérochon. *The Frenetic People*
Pierre Pelot. *The Child Who Walked on the Sky*
Jean Petithuguenin. *An International Mission to the Moon*
J. Polidori, C. Nodier, E. Scribe. *Lord Ruthven the Vampire*
P.-A. Ponson du Terrail. *The Immortal Woman; The Vampire and the Devil's Son; The Police Agent*
Georges Price. *The Missing Men of the* Sirius
René Pujol. *The Chimerical Quest*
Edgar Quinet. *Ahasuerus; The Enchanter Merlin*
Jean Rameau. *Arrival; in the Stars*
Henri de Régnier. *A Surfeit of Mirrors*
Maurice Renard. *The Blue Peril; Doctor Lerne; The Doctored Man; A Man Among the Microbes; The Master of Light*
Restif de la Bretonne. *The Discovery of the Austral Continent by a Flying Man; Posthumous Correspondence* (3 vols.); *The Fay Ouroucoucou* (2 vols.)
Jean Richepin. *The Crazy Corner; The Wing*
Albert Robida. *The Adventures of Saturnin Farandoul; Chalet in the Sky; The Clock of the Centuries; The Electric Life; The Engineer Von Satanas*
J.-H. Rosny Aîné. *Helgvor of the Blue River; The Givreuse Enigma; The Mysterious Force; The Navigators of Space; Vamireh; The World of the Variants; The Young Vampire*
Marcel Rouff. *Journey to the Inverted World*

Marie-Anne de Roumier-Robert. *The Voyage of Lord Seaton to the Seven Planets*

Léonie Rouzade. *The World Turned Upside Down*

Han Ryner. *The Human Ant; The Superhumans*

Henri de Saint-Georges. *The Green Eyes*

Louis-Claude de Saint-Martin. *The Crocodile*

Frank Schildiner. *The Quest of Frankenstein; The Triumph of Frankenstein; Napoleon's Vampire Hunters*

Nicolas Ségur. *The Human Paradise*

Pierre de Selenes: *An Unknown World*

Norbert Sevestre. *Sâr Dubnotal: Vs. Jack the Ripper; The Astral Trail*

Angelo de Sorr. *The Vampires of London*

Brian Stableford. *The Empire of the Necromancers (1. The Shadow of Frankenstein; 2. Frankenstein and the Vampire Countess; 3. Frankenstein in London); The Wayward Muse; Eurydice's Lament; The Mirror of Dionysius; The New Faust at the Tragicomique; Sherlock Holmes and The Vampires of Eternity; The Stones of Camelot* (anthologist) *News from the Moon; The Germans on Venus; The Supreme Progress; The World Above the World; Nemoville; Investigations of the Future; The Conqueror of Death; The Revolt of the Machines; The Man With the Blue Face; The Aerial Valley; The New Moon; The Nickel Man; On the Brink of the World's End; The Mirror of Present Events; The Humanisphere*

Jacques Spitz. *The Eye of Purgatory*

Kurt Steiner. *Ortog*

Eugène Thébault. *Radio-Terror*

C.-F. Tiphaigne de La Roche. *Amilec*

Simon Tyssot de Patot. *The Strange Voyages of Jacques Massé and Pierre de Mésange*

Louis Ulbach. *Prince Bonifacio*

Théo Varlet. *The Castaways of Eros; The Golden Rock.; The Martian Epic* (w/Octave Joncquel); *Timeslip Troopers* (w/André Blandin); *The Xenobiotic Invasion*

Pierre Véron. *The Merchants of Health*

Paul Vibert. *The Mysterious Fluid*

Villiers de l'Isle-Adam. *The Scaffold; The Vampire Soul*

Gaston de Wailly. *The Murderer of the World*

Philippe Ward. *Artahe; Manhattan Ghost* (w/Mickael Laguerre); *The Song of Montségur* (w/Sylvie Miller)